The Boys of '58

R.J. Burroughs

Martin Sisters Publishing

Published by

Ivy House Books, a division of Martin Sisters Publishing, LLC

www.martinsisterspublishing.com

Copyright © 2012 by R.J. Burroughs

ISBN: 978-1-937273-21-7

Fiction

Printed in the United States of America
Martin Sisters Publishing, LLC

DEDICATION

This is dedicated to all the men and women that ever wore the military uniform of the United States of America.

ACKNOWLEDGEMENT

I would like to thank Steven Clayton for his expertise in editing the novel before I was able to send it off. Without his hours of hard work this book may never have been published. Also thank you Mike and Kathy Clayton for your technical support and friendship. Lastly, thank you Lisa Young of Princeton, Ill. for your never ending words of encouragement.

R.J. BURROUGHS

Fiction/Literary

An imprint of Martin Sisters Publishing, LLC

Chapter One

I remember the day that Mary Sue Bailey started carrying a purse. It was on that day that my four friends and I never left each other's sight in the school hallway. None of us would even take a drink from the water fountain without posting watch. She had a habit of walking up to anyone drinking and knocking the fire right out of him with a perfect swing of brown cloth to the gut.

It wasn't that we never left each other's sight most of the time anyway, but we were never as careful as after that day. See, it was after the summer of 1958 and pretty much the only time Jake, Charlie, Gary, Bruce, and I weren't together was when we were asleep at our own homes. That hardly separated us, though. I couldn't count the number of times we spent sleeping at each other's' homes, making use of the couch, floor or anywhere else we could make a palette.

We were like the Musketeers we had read about in school the previous year except there were five of us, each with his own little problems. Jake's family had the most money of all of us, but he seemed the most messed up. There was nothing he wouldn't try. Absolutely nothing. We dared him into all types of trouble and he got us back by bringing us with him. It was that very kind of incident that led us into the trouble we were in at school that year.

Mary Sue was going around telling everyone we were a bunch of losers and our families must be losers too to let us run loose like we did. We'd even heard her whispering stuff like, "If you have any common sense, you just won't talk to that lot at all."

It made us mad because we knew the real reason she didn't like us, and it was all because of Bruce. Mary Sue had asked him to come over for supper one evening and he told her that he would the day his father joined the Gay Liberation Movement. We weren't sure what the liberation movement was, but we sniggered on about it anyway cause we had just seen an article about it while looking through a National Geographic and knew that gays were something none of us wanted to be.

Bruce had gone on telling us what his dad said about the gays when we came to that page. He said that his dad talked about two things, single-handedly whipping the Japanese in WWII and how all gay people lived in New Jersey or the northern states because they were all dead scared of tornadoes. Bruce went on for about fifteen minutes about how his dad would sit back in his chair with his Falstaff beer, saying, "It's a fact, boy. Gay people are scared shitless of tornados. That's why you ain't gonna find none of 'em within a thousand miles of Oklahoma 'cause of them tornados."

Well, he went on for so long about the gays and tornados that when Mary Sue asked him to dinner, it was just something he said. We all got a kick out of it, but she sure didn't and made it known 'round school.

We mulled over ideas for weeks trying to decide what would be a fitting come back for Miss Marry Sue Bailey. Gary wanted to kick her butt, but then Gary always wanted to kick someone's butt and we'd all shake our heads and ignore him every time he'd say it. We knew he was kidding when he talked about kicking her butt. It was one of them cardinal sins to hit a girl. Gluttony, laziness and hitting a girl. We'd make fun of them, tease them until they cried, but we knew better than to touch a girl in a couple different ways. We had a list of no-nos and girls were the top two: hitting a girl, holding her hand, eating liver, and kicking a cat or dog unless it was in self-defense, but there seemed to be a lot of rabid dogs. Rabid dogs were the only thing we were allowed to admit to being scared of 'cause if one of them bit you, we knew there was nothing anyone could do for you except tie you to a very big sturdy tree until you went mad and choked to death on the white foam from your mouth while you were trying to bite someone else.

I remember when I got my good idea about how to get Mary Sue back 'cause it was one of the few times I was for sure alone and got my own time to think over things. Granny sent me to the store to pick up a small can of her beloved Garrett snuff and I gladly went. It wasn't that I wanted to go out, but I sure didn't want her to run out. Granny was nice for a granny when she had that little trickle of snuff running out the corner of her mouth, but don't let that trickle run dry. All hell would break loose and she would keep her flyswatter or big old' three-foot ruler she kept by the kitchen sink real close so that every time I walked by she could give me a hell of a swat to the rear. I asked her why a couple times and her answer was always the same, "Hell, you might not deserve that swat, but before I get another chance you'll do something to deserve it." I learned to not ask questions anymore because the answers wouldn't make much sense. Instead, I just kept my mouth shut about those swats or why she kept a ruler in the kitchen and reminded her when I saw that snuff can getting low.

When I reached the store, I saw Sally Majors coming out carrying a large sack of groceries. That wouldn't have been much of an inspiration before, but Sally had been the talk of the town a few months back. She ran off with the high-school French teacher and got married. She was seventeen and Mr. Baxter was thirty-seven. That was about the biggest thing since the Bible salesman came to town and stole the cash box from the Baptist Church. Seeing Sally's large stomach that day, I just knew she was going to have a baby. She wasn't pregnant, mind you, saying that word was another no-no. Sally was either in the family way, with child, or just going to have a baby. Pregnant was only used for bad girls that lived out of our little town or by the doctor. Seeing her 'in the family way' gave me the perfect idea for paying Miss Marry Sue Bailey back. It came to me in such a flash I forgot all about the Garrett Snuff. I turned on my heels and, in a dead run, started for Charlie's house. About halfway there I remembered the snuff and thoughts of flyswatters and yardsticks came to mind, but there was no turning back now, and the respect I'd get from the guys was worth more than just a couple licks.

Reaching Charlie's house, I banged on the door till the usual greeting came. "Stop that banging you little fart," Charlie's mom said. Everyone was a fart to her. Dumb fart Old fart. Young fart. Stupid fart. Young, no-account fart. That was my favorite.

"Is Charlie home, Mrs. Shaffer?"

"Yes, the little, no-account fart is here," she said, turning to fetch her son who was already headed up behind her.

"What you want, fart-head?" he asked, sidestepping the slap he knew would be coming his way. The fart word was used a lot in his house, but only from his mother. When she heard Charlie or one of us use it, you could bet a slap across the top of your head was soon to follow.

"Have the guys meet at the depot after supper tonight. I think I know a way we can pay Mary Sue back for all the trash she's been spreading about us."

"What you thinking?"

For a second, I was going to tell him, but when you get an idea like that, you can't just waste it; you got to tell everyone at once so they can all talk about how brilliant it was. "Just get the guys together, Charlie."

I guess if I had to pick from all my friends, I'd pick Charlie as my best friend. Not to take away from the others, but Charlie and I spent a lot of time together living so close to one another. Charlie outweighed me by a few pounds, but it wasn't enough to tell if we were standing beside each other. We weighed in together for little-league baseball the summer before and Charlie had weighed in at seventy-eight pounds. I was seventy-six, and he hadn't let me live it down. Placing his hand on my shoulder, he'd say, "Sonny, my boy, you know why I out-weighed you by those two pounds?"

I'd reply, "Cause I do a lot more thinking than you and it just naturally kills my brain cells. Over the years, I must have just lost those two pounds in brain cells."

"Yea right, the truth is my deal is just a lot bigger than yours. That's why it takes me such a long time to go to the bathroom. When you have to work with two pounds of extra meat it just takes a few extra minutes."

"Your exactly right, ol' man! That's exactly right!" And he would give me a little shove.

We all met at the depot just after supper that night, and I explained to the guys what we were going to do to little Miss Bailey tomorrow. It called for us to be able to get out of the house in our best clothes, the clothes we wore to church. The guys thought about it for maybe all of five seconds before deciding it was the best idea I'd ever come up with in my entire life. Gary still wanted to kick her butt, but he decided after thinking about it for a minute longer that it was a well thought out plan.

About five-fifteen the next night, we all met at the funeral home that was about a block away from the Bailey house. Bruce was the last one to arrive. Bruce was always the last one to arrive.

The way he walked up to us wearing that old red OU hat, we knew he had to have gotten into it with his Father. When Bruce did something wrong, his Dad would grab the clippers he'd bought and give Bruce a Mohawk haircut. "This better not get me in no more trouble," he said. That meant his Pops was probably drunk and if he got in any more trouble, he'd have to be shut in and listen to his dad's war stories for the millionth time. "If I have to hear him talk about that Bronze Star or Purple Heart again, I might just go into battle myself and get shot in the hip so I can drink beer all day."

"I just hope like hell we don't end up getting our clothes all messed up," Gary said, ignoring Bruce's talk we'd all heard before.

"Heck, just get ready to run," Jake said, more skipping than walking. He always skipped when he was nervous or afraid, though he'd tried to convince us he was never afraid when we all knew better.

Granny said it was a sin to tell a lie, that a man's word was his bond, but she'd never been taunted by one of the guys. So, when it came to being brave or being seen walking with a girl, it was a better policy to outright lie.

About three weeks before all this Mary Sue business, Jake saw me walking with Rita Hood. It didn't take long for it to get back to all the guys. I lied. I lied big time. I told them that Rita called me a coward cause I was afraid to walk with a girl; that if I would walk her home and let one of the guy see, she would let me see her naked from the waist up. That did it. When the word was naked it trumped everything else. There's no bigger word than naked. It was worth it anyway. Many a night, I lay awake thinking how cute she was, wondering what it would be like to kiss her. I knew it would have to be great; that a kiss from someone like her couldn't be bad. Besides, I wouldn't have a clue if it was bad as I'd never kissed a girl besides Granny, which does not count at all. I was told if you kiss a girl and you start to get excited down there, then you liked her a lot. That sure as heck never happened with Granny, thank God, because, as fast as I was with a lie, I would never be able to come up with a lie for that.

No matter how scared we were though, we all walked into Mary's yard, and I told the guys just to go along with what I said to Mrs. Bailey. They all agreed they would back me to the hilt, each nervous and excited for payback.

I stepped up on the large wooden porch and knocked on the screen door like my Grandmother always told me to knock. "Boy, when you knock on someone's door, knock as if you own the place. Makes you sound like you mean business." I gave it three hard, sharp hits.

There the five of us stood like little angels waiting for either Mrs. Bailey or Mary Sue herself. As the door swung open it was neither of them, but instead Mary Sue's Father. I wanted to tell the guys to turn and run, not because he was one mean so and so, but because he was a deacon at the First Baptist Church: the church our folks made us go to each Sunday morning no matter if we were sick or on our death bed. Every Sunday, Mr. Bailey was there to say hello, to lead the Sunday School in prayer, start and finish, and that was the man that just opened the door.

"What can I do for you boys?" he asks, looking not at one of us in particular, but at the whole twitching group. "If you're here to see Mary, she is eating supper. Maybe you could come back in thirty-minutes and I could let her come out on the porch for a few minutes to talk to you."

At that moment, I wanted to just say, "Thank you," turn around, and leave, but we had come this far and I was committed to saying something or living with nothing but ridicule from my friends for the next fifty or sixty years.

I swallowed the Dentine gum I'd been chewing most all day and said, "Mr. Bailey, it isn't Mary we came to see. It is you, sir." The sir was for respect. I knew to butter him up a little bit before we broke him the news.

"Well, what can I do for you boys? Is it about church?"

"Yes sir, it is in a kind of a way." I took a deep breath and kicked around some invisible dirt on the entrance mat. "Mr. Bailey, we found out Mary is with child. We just wanted you to know that whoever the father is; we are here to become your son-in-law. If you could just ask her to please pick the right one, the rest of us can still make it home for supper."

I'd never seen Mr. Bailey's face twist into such a weird expression. I didn't know whether it was anger or disbelief.

"What did you say to me, boy?" he said in a growling whisper.

There was no way I was going say all that over again. I could barely say it the first time before my knees or my heart gave out. "Sir, I said -"

His voice boomed out like I imagined the voice of God did to Moses all those times in the bible, "She is thirteen. Thirteen you hear me? What in the hell - just what in the hell are you boys talking about?" We could see all the blood had drained out of his face and what replaced it was a look I hoped to never see again. I'd never seen a person be hanged or put in an electric chair, but I could only imagine that the look they would have on their face just before the floor falls or the switch is thrown had to be the look now on Mr. Bailey's face.

This was one time in our young lives that we were scared. We knew we were scared, every one of us. We didn't need anyone to holler let's get out of here. No, all of us were just like those Nazis we had seen on TV marching so perfectly in step. All five of us turned at the same time. I couldn't be sure, but it looked like we all took off on the same foot even, just like them Nazis.

Mr. Bailey, after all those years as a deacon in the church, lost his religion in less time it took him to take a breath.

"Come back here you little sons-of-bitches. Get your little lying asses back here right now. She's just thirteen you little – thirteen. Do you hear me you little bastards?" His screams seemed to barely fade with all the distance we were putting between us. We caught the scariest part as we rounded the corner, "I will call every one of your parents and make sure you're all whipped within an inch of your good-for-nothing lives."

The punishments did come, but nothing our parents did to us was worse than how Mary Sue punished us every day for years after that. Sure, she stopped talking about us to her friends and everyone, but that's the day she started carrying her purse. Swinging that thing straight at our guts became muscle memory to her. To this day, I'm not too sure, but I don't think she carried makeup or money in that bag. I think she only carried rocks about the size of baseballs.

R.J. BURROUGHS

Chapter Two

About two weeks after the incident with Mary's Sue's Dad, we found out there would be a traveling carnival coming to Chickasha, a town about eight miles away from Verden. If there was one thing we boys liked, it was the small carnivals that came around about once a year. We placed softball at the top of our list of likes in those days, but a Carnival could and would break up any game with its rides, the cotton candy, and, best of all, the freak shows: the Snake man, half Snake-half man, or the fat woman with the beard. She really wasn't all that fat. Sure, she was large, but not as big as Misses Harkens who lived next to the old jail at the end of Main Street. The doctor in Chickasha told her to start smoking to curve her appetite. It didn't seem to work. When she walked down the street, you had to get out of her way, because when she got to moving, she had a hard time stopping. If you got in her way, she would more-than-likely knock you down, and if she fell on you; well, you were as good as a goner.

Now, the only thing bad about the Carnival was money. It cost for everything. If a guy didn't have at least five dollars, he would be left out of all the good stuff. That meant the five of us had to raise twenty-five dollars which was almost a whole week's pay for some of the men in town. To us, it was more money than we could get our minds around.

"Well, we could take out a loan from the First," Gary said.

"I can see it now. We guys walk into the bank, ask whoever you ask if we could please borrow *twenty-five dollars*," I said. "'Sure, what do you boys have to put up for security,' will be the first thing they will ask. When we tell them we have five water pistols, a used softball, and several bags of marbles, they'll trip over themselves trying to loan us the money."

We deliberated and came to the decision that none of us had the heart to ask our parents, whose money was already stretched thin, so we decided to come up with a plan of our own.

When Charlie said it was possible he could babysit the Brown's six year old son on Wednesday nights while they were in church, I knew he wanted the Carnival real bad. The first time Charlie watched him; the tyke snuck up on him from behind and hit Charlie in the back as hard as he could with a wooden spoon. Charlie said that by the time he stopped shaking from the spoon hit, the little monster had poured all the sugar into the fish tank, killing five goldfish and some brown fish that looked like a catfish with little red legs.

Nevertheless, he did it and we heard the story the next day.

They were watching a Frankenstein movie on TV, which was unusual for Charlie in itself because he was afraid of his own shadow. While watching the movie, the kid started screaming. Charlie ran into the kitchen, finding the six-year old lying on the floor, a bloody butcher knife lying beside him. Little Matt was screaming, holding his chest as he rocked side to side on the bloody floor.

We all wished we were there at that point, but apparently, seeing the child lying on the floor in such a life threatening situation, Charlie panicked. He ran from the house, screaming at the top of his lungs, "Suicide! The Brown kid committed suicide! Help! Someone! Suicide!" He screamed suicide all the way to the

Wednesday night church service. Throwing open the two large doors, he ran inside, screaming, "My God, Preacher. It's suicide. The kid killed himself. Lord, the kid is dead. He done killed himself."

Mrs. Brown jumped up from the pew where she and her husband were sitting screaming, "My baby. What's happened to my baby," as they took off down the corridor.

When the complete congregation reached the Brown home, everyone pushing and shoving one another to get a better look at the horrible sight Charlie had described, they found the six-year-old sitting on the couch, munching potato chips.

After that fiasco, Bruce said he could help his folks sell vegetables at their roadside stand and Jake had a job sweeping out the train depot. He only earned a dollar a week, though, which left us in a bind. The carnival was to be in town in two weeks, so whatever I came up with had better be soon or we boys would be playing softball or just hanging out instead of going. Several nights, I lay awake wondering what in the world I could do to come up with enough money for me and all the guys to get in and have a good time.

About a week before the carnival was to be in town, I snuck up behind my grandmother and poked a finger into her sides, hollering, "Granny girl." I think she sucked down about half the snuff she had in her mouth.

"Good gosh almighty boy, you near gave me a heart attack," she said, coughing and spitting Garrett snuff. She went right for the flyswatter and took some swipes at me, connecting on a couple of them. "Boy, for the life of me I think you are possessed by the devil at times. I pray most every day that an Angel would swoop down here and touch your heart and little butt, puttin' the fear of God into you. Make you a fine Christian boy."

Hearing that, I finally thought of a plan. I was so excited, I wanted to call them right then and there, but I knew the old woman that ran the switchboard had a bad habit of listening in on most all the conversations that went on in town. It would have to wait.

The next afternoon we all met at the train depot.

Our plan involved the use of Mr. Barton's pet goat. Miss Brandey was a fainting goat and Mr. Barton put a lot of store in her. He spent several hours a week trying to train her. However, after owning her for eight years, he never was able to teach her anything other than not crap in the living room. The rest of the house he didn't really care all that much about, but the living room was for guests.

We needed to use Miss Brandey for our money-making scam, but borrowing her from Mr. Barton wouldn't be that easy. It was a known fact that his wife gave him an ultimatum about four years earlier about his goat, "You either keep that goat outside in her pen and stop spending so much time with her, or you will need to find yourself another wife."

After thinking over what his wife said to him, he answered, "I believe it would be a heck-of-a-lot easier to find another wife than another goat with the smarts Miss Brandey has."

Apparently, that wasn't what she had been hoping to hear from him. She turned and reached into the soapy dish water, pulling out an old porcelain pan, with collard greens still inside and brought it down on top of his old head. Not only did it stun him for a couple of minutes, it bent the pot's handle.

By the time he gathered his senses, she had stormed out of the house, gotten into their old forty-eight ford, and headed for her sister's house in Baxter. She never filed for divorce, but she told him she wouldn't come home until he got Miss Brandey the hell off the property.

To this day, when his social security check comes in, she will show up, get enough money from him to help her sister with the food bill, and head back to her sister's. The first few months she did this, she would always check to see if he had gotten rid of Miss Brandey, but after a while she figured it would never happen.

We walked for an hour that day before we saw Barton's small white house, still not sure just what we would say to Mr. Barton to get him to let us borrow his prized goat. We knew it better be something good or we would be going home empty-handed.

Charlie tried to push open the gate, but it didn't want to give, so he shoved a bit more. Bruce gave him a hand pushing on it and slowly it opened with a grinding sound.

"Now what in the natural-born hell do you boys want?" said Mr. Barton as he walked around the side of the old wooden house.

All five of us turned to face the voice in unison.

"Sir, Mr. Barton, Sir. There has been a lot of talk around Verden these days about your goat. Everyone thinks you gave her up because you are so lonely for your wife to come home," I said, the words rolling off rather smoothly. I just hoped they were headed in the right direction.

"Well, who the hell ever started a rumor like that had to be drinking their bath water," he said, taking a step toward us. "If'n I wanted her back - which let me get it straight right off the bat, I don't - if I did, all I would have to do is put Miss Brandey out in that pen over yonder," pointing off to the distance. "Then she'd come back faster than lick-a-dee-split, and that's a fact boys. From then on, I would have no peace ever again. Let me tell you this," he got real close with a finger up in my face like I'd done something wrong. "Cooking! Just let me tell you about cooking. That woman cooks terrible. She can't make something out of a can. A person just has to heat it up. Ruin it, ruin it, I tell you. I will give her this, she is consistent be it store-bought food or something she has come up with from scratch, it always, without fail, tastes like shit. She bought me a candy bar once, still had the wrapper on it, and yes, it tasted just like shit. Now, mind you, boys, I have no idea what shit tastes like, but I bet it tastes just like her cooking. The smell sure matches in and out," he said, finishing up with a satisfied look about him.

"Well sir, I have an idea how we could prove all them people in town wrong about you, your Misses, and that goat of yours," I said, looking over toward the others with their heads bobbing up and down.

He didn't seem to hear me though. Must have been sometime since he had talked to anyone, because he just continued to talk, looking to each of us. "And clean! My gosh, that woman cleaned all the time. She would empty the ashtray by my chair three, four times a night. Neither of us smoked! They say it is bad for you, but I don't put much store in that. After all, it is just smoke. When we would go visit someone - which we didn't that often because I was afraid she might want to help cook –."

"Sir," I tried to cut into the conversation, which he was having none of.

"Stinking! Did I tell you boy about how bad she stunk at times?" We all stood there, shaking our heads, mouths hanging open.

"Yes boys, did that woman ever stink. I have no idea if it was one of them heredity things some families have, or if'n she just naturally stunk. Come to think of it, maybe her food just *tasted* like shit. Maybe it didn't smell all that bad. Maybe, now thinkin' of it, it was her stinking all that time. I thought it was just the food she was cooking," he said scratching under his chin and looking toward the empty sky. "Had to be, just had to be her."

He got paced around a bit, thinking furiously by the look of things. "When we first got married, I thought I could put up with the smell because she was so darn pretty. After only a couple of nights together, I came to regret going to bed. In the early part of our marriage, I tried to get into bed before her, hoping I could go to sleep before she got there. If'n not, I would be up all night from the smell. I'd start fights just so I could sleep on the couch. My sleeping on the couch all them nights is what has made my back so God-awful-bad nowadays. No boys, if I was to ever take that woman back, I would hope someone or somebody would drag me out in that field over yonder and shoot me like the dog I would have to have become."

I took this as my chance to get a word in, "Mr. Barton, would you like us to walk Miss Brandey to town today while you do your chores. We could parade her around town by the bank and grocery store. That would show people that you hadn't gotten rid of her."

He sat there for the longest time, looking first toward one boy, the next, the next. It seemed like forever before he got to his feet and, without saying a word, turned into the house. We boys didn't know if we should just leave and count it up as experience or knock on his door and try to talk him into it some more.

As we were looking at each other, the screen door opened again. Mr. Barton came out carrying a gun. I didn't breathe. I looked to the others. It looked to me that all their blood had run from their faces. I'd never peed my pants, but if I had, that would have been the time.

"Boys," he said, "this here is a double barrel shotgun. I could shoot that old barn over there, and, I bet, the buck shot from this here gun would just about knock that old barn down. Might not knock it completely down, but you can bet it would blow them two doors off the hinges." He paused for a second, his face as serious as ever.

"I don't know if you boys know it or not, but my goat - I like to call her Miss Brandey and would consider it kindly if you boys would call her that as well - I love Miss Brandey just as if'n she was a youngster of my own. If anyone was to hurt her in anyway, well, I just don't know what I would do or, for that matter, what I would be capable of doing to that person. It is a good thing I have this shotgun to use on them, because I sure wouldn't want to get my hands on them. My hands might do a lot more harm than this shotgun," he said, leaning it up against the side of the door.

"Now, I think you boys seem like fine young lads. I wouldn't think there was a bit of harm in any of you. So as much as I love Miss Brandey, I hate the thought of my old woman wanting to come back here to live. I will let you take her for a walk to town. Mind you though, if anything was to happen to her, I just don't know what I would do."

I looked first to him, then to the field he had talked about, and back to the boys. Their heads were no longer bobbing up and down. Now, they were bobbing side to side, as if telling him, "No Sir, we won't do a thing to harm your Goat, 'cause we know there will be hell to pay on our part."

We walked with Mr. Barton to the back of his old house, trying not to step in any goat crap or bump into any of the junk he had spread around. There were old pieces of a rusty plow, several pieces of hog-wire fence, a pile of dresses I guessed he used as rags, and an old television set.

Miss Brandey was chewing on an old chest of draws. When she saw us, she stopped chewing and walked over to Mr. Barton. He patted her a couple of times on the head and took a long brown leather leash off the nail hanging next to the entrance of his barn.

"She likes it out here in the day-time. Course, I always bring her in at night. Goats don't have much of a chance if a bunch of no-account coyotes come prowling around. They could take her down before a man could pick his nose. No sir, ain't about to leave her out here after dark," he said, hooking the leash to her collar.

Opening the gate and handing the leash to Charlie, he said "Now boys, don't get me wrong. If'n anything was to happen to Miss Brandey, you boys better high-tail the heck out of this county. Better yet, it would be better if'n you left Oklahoma completely, 'cause I will be looking for you. Might not find you in a day or two, or even a week, but if'n it takes me a year or the rest of my life, I'll be finding each and every one of you. Mind you, I have read all them Tarzan books by that Burroughs fellow. Know what them natives did when they put the hurt on someone. Well, think of me as one of the natives," he said, smiling as he headed back toward the house.

Chapter Three

Miss Brandey followed along as if she had been around us all her life. Charlie figured it was because she wanted to get away from crazy Mr. Barton. There might have been some truth to that.

We took our time walking to our Sunday school teacher's house, the site for our plan, more out of fear than anything else. When her house came into view, we slowed down a bit. That in itself should have told us that our plan wasn't completely in the right. I wanted to turn around, take Miss Brandey back, and call the whole thing off, but I didn't know which was worse: the repercussions from Mrs. Whitehead or the other boys.

"What if Mrs. Whitehead's husband is home. Then there will be hell to pay," Bruce said, more to the whole group than to one of us in particular. My mind was a bit more at ease knowing for sure that I wasn't the only one so nervous.

"Well if he is home, I hope you get out of my way, because I plan on running like hell out of here," Charlie said, looking over to Bruce.

"Don't tell me the great and mighty Charlie is scared," Gary said, sharing a hesitant smile with the group.

"Fact is, if I were you guys, I would be just as scared, too."

"Yeah? Why is that? Think an old man like Mrs. Whitehead's husband could outrun ya?" I asked.

"No, you fool, it's because Mrs. Whitehead's husband died a couple of years ago. Don't you guys remember hearing about the man who fell off his tractor plowing his alfalfa field a while back? Tractor ran over him. Cut him plum in half. I heard that before the tractor ran out of gas, it dragged the bottom half of his body four, maybe even five miles, from the top part," Charlie said.

We all stopped. Charlie wasn't smiling a bit. He had a way of spicing up any and all stories he told us, but we remembered about the accident. I hadn't been sure who it had happened to until now.

One time, Charlie told us that his Aunt Betty had taken a great fall, killing her on impact. He said she fell about four-hundred and eight feet to her death; that at the time, it had to be a record of any one woman falling that height to her death, at least in Oklahoma.

When I talked to Charlie's mom a couple of weeks later and told her I was sorry to hear about her sister falling to her death, she informed me in no uncertain words that the fall had not killed her. She only slid out of her rocker after she had a heart attack.

When we reached Mrs. Whitehead's home, we stood outside her knee-high, white fence for a few seconds. I knew the others were stalling. Myself, I had a knot in my stomach that felt about the size of one of the prize Black-Diamond watermelons Mr. Bledsoe raised on his farm just east of town.

"Okay, you guys all know what to do. Try not to screw this up or we will all be up to our necks in holy crap," I said to them as I pushed open the gate.

As I walked the few feet to the three little steps leading up to the porch, I went over everything again and again in my head. I have been told that when someone dies, in a millisecond, their life flashes before their eyes. I sure hoped I wasn't dying because everything I had ever done wrong was flashing before me right then along with all the what-ifs about what I was doing. What if the others got chicken and all of a sudden ran the hell off? What if the goat wasn't really a fainting goat? What if Miss Whitehead knew about Miss. Brandey? What if? What if? What if?

Just as I was about to knock on the door, it opened. "Hi, Sonny Boy." Mrs. Whitehead was looking down at me with a smile. If she could have seen in my head then she would have seen pure air. All I could do was stand there and smile.

"Sonny Boy, is there something I can do for you? Something you need?"

"Sorry Mrs. Whitehead," I finally answered, "but things have happened so fast the last few hours that I am in one of the dazes you talk about in Sunday school."

"What happened, child? Your family okay?" she bent down to come to eye level, though it wasn't a very far trip for the lady.

I stared at the rims of her glasses, trying not to look directly into her eyes. It was a trick I had come up with when I was getting ready to lie. "No, my family is doing just fine. Thank you for asking. It's Charlie, Mrs. Whitehead."

"What's wrong? Is he sick or something? Why does he have a goat?" she asked, looking over my shoulder at him and the goat.

I knew this was it. The next minutes would tell if we were going to the carnival or not. "No mum, Charlie is fine. In fact, he is better than fine. I am so happy to say that Charlie has been touched by the Almighty. Charlie is now a bonafide healer just like them healers that come here with the big tents and all," I said to her in the most sincere voice I could muster up.

"A what?" She stood to look over at Charlie. The change in her eyes gave a vision of me running in the next few seconds.

"Yes mum, a healer. God done come down from way up there above and touched my friend Charlie with the healing power. Fact is I bet he is a better healer than most of the healers with them big tents. Only difference between him and the other men is he doesn't have a tent yet." I said.

"Well of all things, I have heard it all now. Boy, those men that come here do all kinds of good for people with their healing powers."

My grandmother told me the men that come here claiming to be healers from God were a bunch of black-hearts, drunkards, and money-grabbers. I wasn't about to tell her that, though.

"It's true, Mrs. Whitehead. We were all shooting marbles when, all-of-a-sudden, Charlie got a God awful look on his face for a couple of seconds. He started talking in some strange language none of us ever heard before. Then he went to shaking like he was gonna freeze to death. I was about to run for help, 'cause I figured he was going to pass away right there and then, but before I could get up and get going, he stopped shaking. This smile came to his face. It was such a calm smile that it settled us guys right down.

"What?" I haven't seen anyone look so confused since Jake got kissed by a mob of girls last year.

"I sure know it's hard to believe, but, when that smile came to his face, he looked at us and said, 'Fellas, I have been touched by an angel. An angel of God done told me that I have the power of life and death in my hands."

"No. No. That can't happen. Only God himself has the power of life and death. I think Charlie's lying to you boys and you all need to go on home." I could tell she didn't believe anything I was telling her, and that she was about to turn around to go back into the house.

"I know it is hard to believe, him being young like he is and all, but it is sure enough a fact. That is why we came to you, being our Sunday School teacher and all. We knew if anyone could tell us just what was up, it would be you sure enough." I said, hoping to make to make her feel more like we needed help and less like we were committing what she had called blasphemy or whatever.

"Charlie said the Angel told him he would only have the power of life and death over dumb animals until he got grown. Then he could only use his healing power, because the power of death was only God's. God was only letting him use it at this time just so he could prove himself to non-believers."

"And I am supposed to believe this?"

"No. We don't expect anyone to believe it, 'cause Charlie was the only one to see that angel. He had to prove it to us, and the only reason he did that is because we teased him so much about it. Charlie said the angel told him to keep quiet about his powers until he was older, but he could show only people that was in real good with God himself. That is when we thought of you. That is why we have the goat. We wanted to show you the power Charlie done got from that angel," I said, smiling at Charlie and the others.

That was the sign. They came walking up with Miss Brandey, stopping a few feet from the steps.

"Charlie, Mrs. Whitehead would like to see the power that angel gave you." The moment of truth was upon us. If Mrs. Whitehead knew about fainting goats, we were up the creek with no paddle. If Miss Brandey didn't do her part, it would be the same.

Charlie raised his hands into the air and let his eyes roll back into his head, screaming, "You goat, with the power I was given by that angel of God, I evoke death to you. Die, sinner goat.

Just like clockwork, Miss Brandey's legs became stiff as boards, her back and neck went rigid, and she fell straight over. There she lay on her side, looking as if she had been dead for weeks.

Looking back as Mrs. Whitehead, the expression on her face was hard to figure out. She let out a little sound, more of a gasp than anything else. I thought she was going to follow Miss Brandey and faint too, but then a grin took over, a big one. I was afraid she might hurt her mouth, smiling so wide.

Charlie went into the next part of his routine as I winked at him. "Goat, I give life back to you. I give to thee life eternal. Now rise goat. Rise and go frolic with your goat friends," he said much more softly, leaning down to stroke Miss Brandey.

Not more than a second or two after he laid his hand on Miss Brandey did she make a small kick with her back legs. Before you could blink an eye, she was up and chewing grass in Mrs. Whitehead's front yard.

That was all it took. Mrs. Whitehead leaned against the door post and slid down, praising first this angel, then God, then back to the angel, back to God.

I tried for several seconds to talk to her, but she was too busy praising and praying to everyone she could think of up in the sky. I kind of felt bad for her as I watched her sitting on her butt, tears running from both eyes.

After several minutes, she composed herself and called Charlie to her. When he came up, she grabbed him and kissed him near a million times on top of his head. She couldn't see the faces he was making at us boys as she kissed and hugged him. It was better that way, 'cause he was happier than I had seen him in a long time.

"What can I do for you, Charlie? What can I do for you, you gifted child? Name it. Let me do something for such a blessed child," she said, kissing his head between each word.

"What we felt we should do, Mrs. Whitehead, now that Charlie has the gift of healing, would be for us to give money to the church to show out thanks. We wondered what you thought about that and if you had any old bottles we could cash in for church money. We are hoping to raise twenty-five dollars," I said, taking the lead back from Charlie before he did anything we'd regret.

I'd never seen an old woman from the church jump so fast and high. She must have come a centimeter from the door frame above her.

Charlie started to say something to us, but I put a finger to my lips. All we needed was for him to say something stupid loud enough for her to hear.

Mrs. Whitehead appeared as fast as she disappeared. I could see she had some money in her hands. "Here you go, Charlie. I believe it is the right thing to do to give a tithe to the church as you have been blessed by God as no other," she said, placing a hand on Charlie's head. "Take this with my blessing, child."

When Charlie and the others saw the two twenty dollars bills and one ten, I thought they would scream with delight, but none of them did.

"Mrs. Whitehead," I said, "we better take this goat back to its home. It might need rest. I'm sure it takes a lot out of you being dead one second and alive the next," I said stepping off the porch, hoping the others would follow suit.

She didn't say a word, just stood there, nodding.

Walking away, I whispered to Charlie, "Thank her for the money, you fool."

Holding tight to the money, he turned, "Mrs. Whitehead, I thank you for the church money, and when I get older, if you was to catch the cancer or get something that could kill you, I will come right away and heal the heck out of you, your family members as well. Wish I could have been here when your husband got run over and killed, 'cause I would have sure fixed him right up," he said, hollering back as we walked quickly away.

"Shut the hell up," I said to him in a low voice, knowing he'd screw up if he was given another second, just as I had first expected.

We skipped all the way back to Mr. Barton's house. None of us had ever seen fifty dollars before. We had enough for the Carnival and a whole lot more.

Charlie wanted to buy a bunch of food and spend a few days camping in the foothills.

Gary wanted to buy a bunch of candy and crap as he liked to say and go to the Johnny Mack Brown Movie that was playing. Bruce wanted to buy another baseball mitt, the pocket in his old glove having a hole in it about the same size as a softball. Every time he used it, he had to wear four pair of socks over his mitt hand with the toes of the socks cut out so it didn't sting so badly.

Jake wanted to spend his extra five dollars trying to find out if Sally Sparks, the woman living two doors down from the old jail was really a hooker or not.

I just wanted to save the money for our next adventure, whatever that may be, but "saving money" was not in the guys' vocabularies.

I never did find out what the guys spent the extra money on, I just know they did spend it because in a couple of days everyone needed money to get into the movie.

My extras were gone as well. I gave them to my grandmother, because in those days we seemed to always be short on money when we needed little things like milk or bread.

We boys took in the carnival when it came to town. When we heading home, Bruce said it all when he said, "That was the best time ever and no harm done."

Mrs. Whitehead never made mention of it at any time, but she would look at Charlie with a big smile and a wink each time she saw him. That kind of creeped us out, but we knew she just thought, as that long as Charlie was around, there would be no need to worry about the common cold, much less a heart attack or the dreaded cancer.

Chapter Four

Now, Jake was surely the most gullible of us all. We exploited this to the point that, at one point, he had to ask, "Okay, is this truth or crap," every time we started talking.

Walking along a dirt road one day, doing nothing as usual, Jake started telling us about his Uncle Collin. He told us that his Uncle worked on a dairy farm somewhere up North, and that he was some kind of professional runner, hoping to one day get a chance to try out for the eight-eighty high hurdles. Of course, we were all baffled as to what in the world made him think of his uncle Collin.

"Those cows over there," he said, pointing at a large bunch of white-faced cows about one-hundred yards away.

"For God's sake, how do white-faced cattle make you think of your Uncle? Is he that big of a guy," drawing a chuckle from the guys.

"He lives up North in Minnesota just a couple of miles from the Canadian border," he said.

"So…"

"My Uncle told me they play a game up there kinda like our dare game. The only difference is it's called nut slapping," he said, smiling at no one in particular.

Mind you, I had played a lot of I dare you and a lot of double dare you, though I seemed to always end up on the wrong end of the dare. Last year, Charlie double dared me to slap Miss Townsen on the butt in homeroom. I knew I would be getting a couple of licks from Mr. Fix, but it was something I had to do if I wanted to hold my place as the more or less leader of our little bunch.

When the bell rang, I took my time walking out, made it look like I was hunting something in my desk. Usually, I was the first one out the door, but when the usual kids were crowded around the exit, I made my move. Walking up behind her, I screamed as loud as I could, "Black Widow," and slapped her on the butt. I heard the sound of the slap, the scream, and as she turned, her eyes met mine.

In a final act of desperation, I pushed a couple of the girls out of the way, screaming, "Watch out! Spider!" I didn't see the anger in her eyes, but I was told about it later.

My hands were feeling the places that the paddle had hit so many times when Jake brought me to the present.

"Well, according to my Uncle Collin, it is a game of courage they play where he is from. What you have to do is walk up behind a bull, slap him on the nuts with your naked hand - you can't wear a glove, use a stick, anything like that - then you have to get away before he can get to you."

"That's impossible," Bruce said. "First of all, he would see you coming and attack you or run away first."

"That what I said, but Uncle Collin said if you walk straight up behind him while the other people keep his attention, it works every time," Jake said looking at me for support. I had none.

"Seems like a mighty fine way to get killed or at least get the crap stomped out of you. No one in his right mind would ever walk up behind a bull and slap him on the nuts. It's just something people shouldn't do with their minds about them," I said as I started walking on, hoping that would be the end.

"Piece of cake," Charlie said.

Should have known it would never get past Charlie. Something like this was right down his alley - maybe a challenge.

"Charlie, that bull will kill you," I said, pointing toward the big black bull standing about a hundred yards in the field. It looked to me to be about the same size as the old Packard the postman drove.

"No problem. You guys just get in front and keep his attention until I can get behind him in his blind spot. I'll do the rest. I'm going in," Charlie said, walking up to a fence post he could use to step over the barbed wire.

We knew there was no way we could change his mind. He was committed now. We'd never let him live it down if he changed his mind now, and he knew it. The only thing we could do now was try to help him.

Bruce and Jake went a couple of hundred yards down the road, and then cut into the field with the cattle. The cows paid them no heed, walking away if they got close to one of them. Jake and Bruce walked slowly toward the bull, keeping the fence close enough for an easy escape. The bull started walking slowly toward them, keeping his head down, feeling a threat of some kind.

All this time, Charlie was slowly walking, creeping up behind it. When Charlie was about fifteen feet behind the bull, Jake started waving his arms in the air, hollering, "Bull. Over here, bull. Over here." The bull stopped in his tracks, figuring out the boys' purpose. Just as it started kicking up dirt with it right leg, Charlie made his move. He ran the last four or five feet behind the bull, sliding down on this left knee as he struck.

I couldn't hear the thud when he struck the bull's nuts, but I could see the back of the bull leap from the ground, its two back legs coming completely off the ground. While its hind legs were still in the air, it turned on Charlie. I never thought a bull could scream, but I swear I heard something like it drowned in the snorting. Charlie was already up and running when the bulls back legs hit the ground.

I'd never seen something so big move so fast. For all that Charlie was running, the bull was gaining. Just as he was about ten feet from the fence, the bull struck. Its large head went under and between Charlie's legs. With one swift, upward thrust, Charlie was air born. The first half of his body cleared the barbed wire fence, but from the waist down he wasn't so lucky. I could hear his jeans ripping in several places.

When he landed in the ditch, the wind was knocked completely out of him. All he could do was lie there, breathing, moaning, and smiling each time he tried to take a breath. He knew he'd be able to show those scars for a very long time.

Chapter Five

We had a friend in those days named Joe. He didn't hang around with us all that much. Everyone in town thought he was mentally challenged. We boys knew better. Sure, he was strange, real strange, but mentally challenged, no.

Joe had lost a finger when he was ten years old. Seems he was working on the lawn mower one afternoon, pulling all the old grass away from the wheel that had accumulated over the year. His older brother, Buck, thought it would be funny to give the little mower a quick push, scare the crap out of Joe.

While Joe was squatting next to the mower, Buck snuck up behind him and gave the mower a quick push forward, then jerked it back. When the mower was pushed forward, his finger on his right hand was cut and mangled between the blades. Jerking the mower back sliced the finger off just as neat as you please. I wasn't there; however, I was told that Joe didn't scream or make a sound. He just looked up at Buck and straight back down to his severed finger. He picked up his finger and walked into his house to show his mother. Big Buck had passed out from the site of blood.

Walking in carrying a severed finger is just about enough to cause a major heart attack which his Aunt Bessie promptly did when she saw what happened to the boy.

Luckily, his Uncle Burness, father, and mother were all in the kitchen. Hearing Aunt Bessie fall against the small coffee table made them all come a running.

Joe's mom could not find anything handy to wrap his hand in. She shuffled him to the bathroom and wrapped his hand and arm in female napkins.

Together, they loaded Aunt Bessie, Joe, and Buck, who had just come back from walla walla land, into their old rust and green Dodge pick-up and headed out. Must have been a heck of a sight, seeing them drive to the hospital in Anadarko, Joe's mom fanning Aunt Bessie for all she was worth, screaming, "Wake up, woman. Wake up," Joe holding his arm wrapped in all those female napkins up as high as he could, and Buck leaning over the tailgate tossing up everything he had eaten the last couple of days.

They admitted Aunt Bessie to the hospital and then let her go the next day, deciding it wasn't a heart attack, but they couldn't put Buck all the way back together. The doctor placed the severed finger in a bunch of gauze, smiled, and said, "Boy, you're lucky. You will never have to go to war. They don't send men to war that don't have no trigger finger." Only person in the room that got a kick out of that was the doctor himself. When he realized no one in the room was laughing, he stopped and said, "Bring him back in a couple of days."

When they all got back in to the pick-up, Joe jumped out and ran back into the hospital to pick his finger out of the old trash can. That summer, we invited Joe to go camping with the rest of us. The look on his face told us he thought we were just joking with him as so many of the kids in school did. When he finally decided we really wanted him to come along, his grin was a mile wide. I guess there wasn't all that many people in town that paid that much attention to Joe, not in a good way.

When we all showed up at Charlie's house to head to the river, some of us brought food, couple of the others brought canteens full of water. Joe brought four buttercups, six pieces of bubble gum, a pocket knife with no blade, and four plumbs. I got onto him for not bringing more, but he said he didn't have enough room in his pack.

"Why? It's the same size as mine," I said to him.

Reaching in, he pulled out an old mason jar with several green beans. Floating among the green beans was his severed finger.

"Why in the name of Jupiter did you bring that thing?" I asked him.

"My mother said she was going to toss it out whenever she got the chance. I won't be giving her that chance," he said, holding the jar up higher for all of us to see.

When we got to a spot that looked good for camping, we set up our small tent and did a little fishing. A little because Bruce got his little red and white cork caught on a branch at the edge of the river.

Sliding down the bank to un-snag it, he reached out a little bit too far and fell stomach-first into the slow moving, rust-colored water. That was pretty much the day. That night, we all set around telling stories, talking about what we hoped to be in the years to come. Around midnight, we all decided to turn in, five boys sleeping in a tent made for no more than three.

We had barely laid down when we heard coyotes. We boys all lay in our sleeping bags, looking from one to the other. Joe said, "Sounds like they are getting closer."

No one answered him. I saw Joe clutching the jar of green beans and his finger as close as he could to his chest.

"You know, I don't know all that much about wild animals, but I do know that they always come to where the food is," said Charlie.

"That's makes it easy enough. Let's just throw the food in the river," I said to no one in particular.

"Yeah, let's do that," Gary answered without hesitation, "but then who's to do it?"

Without a word being said, Jake was up out of his sleeping bag, gathering up all the food we had in the tent. He crawled to the small opening of the tent, sticking only his head out. When he decided it was now or never, he crawled out of the tent. He threw the food, piece by piece as hard as he could toward the river. I guess to make it even better, he threw the little pan we used to cook, the knives, and the forks into the water as well.

We could hear everything as it hit the water with a distance splash.

Crawling back into the tent, he said, "Okay, boys. That's the way a marine would do it."

"Hell no! A marine would have gone out there and kicked the hell out of anything in the area," Jake said.

There was only a slight breeze, just enough to make little dark squiggly lines on the wall of the tent from the shadows coming from the tree line. There would be no sleep for any of us that night.

"I think the sound is getting closer," Jake said.

"For true, crap almighty," Charlie said

. "Did you throw everything in the river?" I asked Jake.

"I threw everything I could get my hands on. Crap, I would have thrown this tent in if it had not been staked down."

What seemed like hours couldn't have been more than a couple of minutes. I wasn't sure what was going on in the other boys mind's, but I could see myself being torn limb to limb by a bunch of wild beasts of some strange unknown nature.

"My god. It's the green beans and Joe's finger they smell," Bruce screamed in a whisper.

Screaming in a whisper is like screaming as loud and as hard as you can, only the words come out in a whisper, something we boys mastered years before by spending the night with one another. Many times my grandmother would scream at us boys from her bedroom that if we didn't quiet down, she was going to come in and beat us within an inch of our lives. We'd learned quickly how to scream and laugh out loud in a whisper.

We all turned to look at Joe lying in the fetal position, clutching that stupid quart jar with his legs drawn up to cover what he could of the jar.

"Joe, we got to get rid of that stupid finger," Charlie whispered to him loud enough for all of us to hear.

Joe didn't answer with words, but his shaking his head so violently back and forth let us know what he thought of our plan in no uncertain terms. No.

"Joe, it's either that finger in the river, or all of us will die. Just the plain simple truth, we will all die. Then where will we be? Dead. That's sure enough where we will be. Dead," Gary said.

There was no convincing Joe. All he could do was lay there, shaking his head from side to side.

I kinda felt sorry for him. I knew that finger meant something to him. What it was I didn't know. Maybe he thought that someday he would be able to get it reattached, but for now it was about to get us all killed in a way that no man should die, being attacked by wild, vicious Coyotes.

As if we boys had been planning this attack from birth, when I made a move toward Joe, the others followed suit. I grabbed for the green bean jar and, at the same moment, Charlie reached over the lying boy, taking hold of both his arms. While Bruce grabbed one leg, Jake got the other, and Gary helped me pry Joe's fingers from the death grip he now had on the jar.

"No, don't damned you. Damned you," Joe screamed at us, not a whisper scream at all. I couldn't believe a boy could make such a noise. It was like we were the coyotes tearing away the finger like it was part of his hand still.

With Gary's help, I slid the jar out of his grip. I wanted to hand it to Charlie and let him pull his marine act again as I had no desire to go outside the tent to face whatever might be out there. I knew, though, that it was up to me with the way the others were still fighting with Joe, trying to control his thrashing about.

Sliding out the little opening in the tent, I stood up as quick as possible to find if the killer Coyotes had arrived. I took two large steps toward the river and threw the jar as best as possible. While it was still in flight toward the river, I jumped back into the tent.

Joe had stopped thrashing about somewhat, and was more or less crawling back toward the wall of the tent. Through the dark, I saw a face that could kill poking out from the tent.

He just sat there, looking at me. I looked back at him and wanted to explain to him how we had just saved his life by getting rid of that green bean covered finger.

I couldn't believe he just stared, never once blinking his eyes. I no longer felt sorry for him. I felt sorry for myself, because I knew in his mind that it was I that he was concentrating all his anger toward.

That God awful stare was saying, Sonny I am going to get you, maybe not tonight, maybe not tomorrow, maybe not even this month or this year, but I am going to get you someday. Sometime, I will fix you for what you just did.

As I crawled back into the tent, keeping my distance, I could see the hope in everyone but Joe's face that I had detoured the coyotes, but my sureness was only briefly enjoyed. We heard them just outside the tent. When one of them would walk by outside, the moon would cast their shadows against the side of the canvas tent.

We boys gathered together in the middle of the tent, hoping to draw on strength from one another, all but Joe. He set at the side, staring at me, oblivious to anything going on around him other than the anger he now felt for me.

When the little flap that covered the entrance to the tent started to move inward, I felt just a little pee, start to run down my leg. I screamed as loud as I could in unison with the others when the flap flew back.

Three of the largest coon hounds I had ever seen came storming into the tent, licking each one of us in turn. I believe the dogs were as glad to see us as we were afraid to see them.

Looking over at Joe, the dogs just seemed to enrage him even more. I believe he was hoping they had been coyotes. Hoping before they got to him that he would be able to watch them devour the person that separated him from his finger.

Chapter Six

Kathy was a likeable girl. Her only problem was that she liked to get people in trouble. She would go to great lengths to do so, having no problem going out of her way if there was the slightest chance she could cause problems. If you wanted to pass a note in class, it better not touch her hand. If she got a hold of it, you can bet it would be opened and read. She always came up with the excuse that she thought the note was to her, but no person in his right mind would ever write her a note.

About three weeks after my incident, she intercepted a note from Neil Arron going to Jake. It said, *Boy, Sally sure has on a tight sweater today, too bad there isn't anything under it, ha ha.* Most all notes ended in ha, or dumb ass. She told her immediately and the looks between the four of them were a mix of embarrassment at the situation and anger at Kathy.

Kathy met Neil at the door after class, wanting to know what he meant by it. Course, she knew what he meant. She only wanted to make him sweat a little before she stuck the knife into him.

Neil skirted the issue with "ums" and "ahs" as much as possible before he finally blurted it out, "Boobs. I was talking about boobs, okay?"

Kathy acted as if she was completely taken by surprise by the word "boobs," but she knew all the time what he meant, and she knew all the time what she was going to do.

"Well, Neil Arron, you should be ashamed of yourself. That is the nastiest thing I think I have ever heard a boy say. I better give this note to the teacher, because I sure don't want any part of it. I sure don't want my name associated with it in anyway."

"Come on, Kathy. Just give it to me, and I will tear it up, no big deal."

"No. Just as soon as I gave it back to you, you would think you could pass notes like that again. Who's to know? You may even say stuff like that about me. I could never be sure you wouldn't," she said, smiling a tiny bit and having the time of her life at Neil's expense.

"No. No, Kathy. I would never say anything like that about you," he more or less pleaded to her.

"Why? You think I don't have boobs now or something?" she asked him, purposefully placing a frown on her face.

"I didn't mean anything of the such. I just meant you are so nice and things like that."

"Well I think I better give it to the teacher, be shut of the whole mess," she answered him.

"Come on, Kathy. There has to be something I can do, something to make this right," going down on two knees.

Kathy put a finger to her right temple as if she was trying to think, then under her chin, looking first this way then the other. "Tell you what I will do. If you will walk me home after school and carry my books, then when we get to my house I will give you the note. I know that will make you think twice before you try to degrade another woman," she said.

If you could have seen the look on Neil's face as she was telling him this, you couldn't have helped feeling sorry for him. When she said, "and you have to hold my hand all the way," though, that was the part I thought should have done him in.

I know if this had happened to me, joining the United States Marines, as tough and mean as they say their boot camp is, would have seemed like the better option. Before I would have walked her home, holding her hand, I would have tried to move to the river to live the rest of my life out eating grass and fish.

As shocking as it was though, Neil did as she asked him. I guess he was more afraid of the teacher or what the teacher might say to his parents. After that day, he was never the same. Something must have happened in that short walk, because as much as we teased him, he continued to walk with her. One good thing did happen from that: when Kathy was passed a note, she just passed it on. We boys thought she must have gotten what she wanted all along, Neil.

Chapter Seven

That was about the last thing that happened before we all broke for summer break. This was always the time that our mischief hit its beautiful prime.

One day, a couple weeks after our freedom began, we were all standing outside the grocery store, talking to Mr. Podolak and drinking our RC Cola. I have no idea how the subject ever came up, but it was a subject we boys were more than interested in. We were all talking about ghosts and places in Oklahoma that were haunted.

"Boys, did you ever hear about the hatchet-killer we had in these parts 'bout seventy-five to say fifty years ago?" he said, looking at each of us in turn.

Now, when anyone says hatchet and killer in the same sentence, you automatically have our attention. I believe either one of those words by themselves would do the trick. Together, though, we were mesmerized.

"No," we all said together.

Mr. Podolak was an old man. He looked to me to be in his eighties; however, I was sure no judge of age.

I thought Miss Jackley, our geography teacher was an old woman ready to retire. When I asked her how much longer until she could retire, she said, "Twenty years," hateful-like. "I'm only thirty years old. Now sit down and read your geography book."

Mr. Podolak really did look old, though. I wouldn't want to tell him, but he looked like he was on his last breath. I hadn't seen all that many dead people at my age, but I had however seen a lot of dead animals. Some of them looked a lot better than he did.

"Let me tell you the story, boys," he said, moving to the small green bench just to the left of the door. Grabbing hold of the back of the bench with both hands, he sat down. It sounded like every bone in his body was breaking as his butt slowly came to rest on the bench. I wanted to reach out to help him, but I was afraid I might do more damage than help. The way his skin hung off his arm, I was sure there was a good chance it could come off in my hand with very little effort.

"Now, don't get me wrong. I was a boy 'bout you boys' age when I first heard this story."

As he talked, we moved a little closer. Don't know why, but when a person is telling you something about ghosts, dead people, or killers, you need to get as close to them as possible.

"Boys, it's like this. Seems several years ago, young people didn't have no TV like they do today. At night, you had to do with what you had to entertain yourselves. A lot of young'uns read, but most just played in the yard until time for bed.

"Anyways, the boys and girls of courting age liked to go to the old river bridge and sit around there. I guess they watched the moon light reflect off the water. For me, I sure as heck don't understand that one little bit. All the years I have been living on this old Earth, in this old town, I have not once seen that river look nothing other than the same old brown, muddy way it looks today. I guess they had a bench somewhere down there by the bridge. Best I can recall, it's that little cleared out spot just off to the west side of the bridge. I'm sure you boys have seen it."

Looking at one another, we all nodded our heads yes. In fact, that was the spot we liked to fish from. It was right close to the water. If you needed to pee, it wasn't but a few feet to the other side of the bridge, a nice safe place to take care of business.

"Anyways, there was this young couple. I think the boy's name was," Mr. Podolak got quiet for a couple of seconds, looking up at the empty sky. "Let's see. The girl's name was Donna Harp. Ah! If you boys can believe it, the boy's name was Curt Harp. Believe me, there was some of that talk about incest that went around this here town. A lot of the town folks hereabouts wouldn't even talk to them kids. I guess they thought they were brother and sister or, at very least, cousins."

"You heard talk around town that if them two Harp kids got married and had young'uns; more likely than not, the young'uns would be born with a couple fewer fingers. You boys being as young as you are, it wouldn't be fittin' me for to tell you all the names and bad things that was said about them two kids," he pulled some tobacco and papers out of his pocket to roll a cigarette.

As he was putting together the making of his cigarette, he said, "It got so bad around these parts that Mrs. Harp, the girl's mother, went to a town meeting and gave all the people attending the what for. She told them that her daughter was no more kin to Curt Harp than Mr. Goel was to his nasty, old pig.

"She explained in a harsh way that Curt just happen to have the same last name as Donna. Donna's ancestors were part English and Choctaw Indian. Meanwhile, Curt's ancestors were of German and French decent. She said that if she heard any more about this incest or babies born looking queer, then she would be taking the broom to the individual doing the talking. She'd beat them like they were some step-kid of a wife-beater."

Rolling the makings between his fingers, he went on saying, "Believe you me that shut up a lot of the talk that went on around here. People were sure Mrs. Harp meant every word about that old broom of hers."

"Getting back to it, most all summers you could find Curt and Donna Harp sitting down next to the bridge. They were all cuddled up like a couple of bear cubs, watching that old muddy water flowing by. I guess at their age that was some kind of a big deal. An old log floating by must have been real excitement to them," he said, snickering to himself. He thought he said something real funny and paused for some laughing agreement.

"Go on. Go on," Gary said.

"What next?" Charlie and Bruce chimed in together.

"Well, one Saturday evening 'bout ten-thirty, I was told, Mrs. Harp - that would be Curt's Mother, not Donna's - came to town. She was asking if anyone had seen her boy. A couple of the old men sitting around whittling or doing whatever shook their heads. Heck, they could have been setting on this here bench," Mr. Podolak said, touching the bench with the hand not holding his cigarette. I couldn't help but wonder how long it'd take him to light that thing.

"Well, Mrs. Harp was in a real titter. She knew the kids liked to go to the river and spoon, so she asked the men to lend a hand," he said. "The two men sitting on the bench - I never did find out their names - said they would go down to the river and check on the two Harp kids. The men must've figured the two just got tied up in their spooning and forgot the time."

Taking an old match out of his breast pocket, he handed it to Gary for him to light his cigarette. I guess he was afraid he might set himself on fire if he tried to light his own smoke.

Gary held the lit match up to his cigarette, and Mr. Podolak took a long drag on it. "Well, them two men sent Mrs. Harp on home then headed straight down to that bridge. When they got to the river, neither man had a light of any kind. I heard that all they had were several matches like that one there," he said, pointing at the burnt match Gary still held in his fingers.

"Lighting one of the matches, they made their way down to the bench that the kids always sat in to do their kissing and such. However, there was no sign of the two at all. The bench did have what looked to them as blood all over it. They were sure someone had used it to clean a catfish, but when there was no fish skin anyplace to be found. They got a little worried.

"They were getting ready to leave and tell someone about what they had seen when one of them noticed a small red pocket book lying real close to the water's edge. Moving over to pick it up, the guy that saw it first let out a God awful scream. I've been told it was so shrill and gut wrenching that it caused the other man to wet himself right there on the very spot. Seems lying there, half in half out of the water, was Donna Harp.

"It wasn't just the body that caused the shriek, though. They knew it was her from it being her and Curt's spot. What had caused the gut wrenching scream was, when the first man pulled a little bush aside to see her face, her head was as good as gone. Where her head should have been, there was only a drooping neck that was dripping dark river water." Mr. Podolak said shivering as he took a long drag off his smoke.

"They knew Curt's body had to be close by, because he would never let this happen to his girlfriend without putting up one hell of a fight. I heard they said that they wanted to search for the body, but they knew they had better let the law know before they destroyed anything that might help find the killer or killers. However, I believe them two men were done scared shitless, couldn't wait to get the heck out of there. Besides that one fellow needed to get into some dry pants. It wouldn't do at all to run to town telling folks what you just found with pee all over you."

Throwing what was left of his cigarette into the street over Gary's head, he went on with his story, "They got Donna's body, or what was left of her body, out of there the next morning. Town folk spent several days hunting for the boy's body or the poor girl's head and had no luck at all on either account.

"Stories went around this town like wild fire. They said things like, the killer murdered the boy and weighted his body down, tossing him into the river. They figured catfish and perch ate the whole thing.

"Some people thought Curt asked Donna to get married, and she laughed and said no. Must've made him so mad that he killed the heck out of her right then and there, cutting her head off to take with him while he ran from the law. I guess he didn't have no picture of her. Her head must have been the next best thing. Myself, I would have thought a boy carryin' a girl's head would make a hell of a spectacle, but then what do I know." he said looking at me.

"Well, the truth is, her head was never found, and Curt was never seen again. To this day, if a person goes down there around midnight and is real quiet, they can see Donna Harp's ghost in her white and yellow polka-dot dress, looking for her head. I have even been told that there have been sightings of Curt's ghost calling out Donna's name," Mr. Podolak said.

As he started his long process of getting back on his feet, we were already looking to one another, well aware of what needed to be done that very night.

Chapter Eight

That evening, we all met at my home after supper. Bruce was even there on time, as hard as it is to pull him away from food. He could eat more than two full grown men, yet never seemed to gain weight. My grandmother said it was because he was such a nervous type. "Gosh all mighty, that boy does some of that worrying," she'd say.

Setting at the store earlier, talking about ghosts, we'd decided what we would need for that night.

Charlie thought the wooden cross his folks kept in their bedroom would repel ghosts until we convinced him that crosses were only made to drive away vampires. Any self-respecting ghost would only laugh at a boy carrying a wooden cross.

Bruce said his father kept a couple of machetes in the old milk barn behind his house. I had to explain to him that a ghost was hollow or more like a cloud. If you hit a ghost with a machete, it would only go through them like spit through air and make them angrier.

Gary thought that if we took a bunch of flowers, we could make peace with the ghost right off the bat.

"How did you ever get such a stupid idea?" Jake asked.

"Stands to reason," Gary said, "when someone dies, people send flowers. When my Aunt Sara died, it smelled like the South American rain forest."

"South American rain forest, my big, fat foot. You ain't never been out of town more than twenty miles, and you're talking about smelling like a rain forest?" Charlie said to him.

"I may not have been out of Verder all that far, but I seen the rain forest many a time in National Geographic," he said, grinning ear to ear.

"You sure enough might have done that, but you sure didn't smell no rain forest from any book. That's a darn fact," Bruce said.

"The real reason for all the flowers is to hide the smell of death," Jake said.

"Now what are you talking about? The smell of death?" I asked.

"Well, when someone dies, there is this smell that they put off. You can smell it as far away as four hundred to five hundred feet; it is the smell of death. My mom went to a friend's house once to take some chicken or something, because they were expecting my mom's friend's mother to pass on right quick. They didn't have time to do no cooking, staying by the bed and all. Well, when mom got home, she said there was this smell of death all through the house," Jake said.

None of us knew anything about death, so we just kind of dropped the subject.

I didn't know that much about ghosts either, but I did know that in order to be a ghost, you had to die. You *had* to be dead. That's why a ghost is a ghost in the first place. Most people go to heaven straight off - kind of like one second you're sitting there eating supper, and the next second you are dead. I wasn't even sure if it took a whole second or not.

I figured if you were killed by someone that didn't like you all that much or slipped from a tall building - any death other than a death when your family is all gathered by your bedside waiting for you to die - than you became a ghost. You have to just kind of walk or float around until you get your paper work ready to get into heaven.

We hadn't actually decided on anything to bring to protect ourselves, but we'd agreed that we would tell our folks we were going to camp out in Gary's back yard. We did that a lot in the summer months so it was a good cover. Then, at about eleven thirty, we would head to the river to the spot where Mr. Podolak said they'd found Donna Harp's body in the water. That would put us boys there only a few minutes before midnight.

We lay in Gary's backyard telling ghost stories, making fun of one another, and talking about how we couldn't stand girls.

When we finally headed toward the river, we had to walk down the deserted sidewalk, straight through town. That in itself was enough to give boys our age the creeps.

Then, all-of-a-sudden, Charlie screamed out, "Wait! Look, look here," he said pointing to the sidewalk.

The way we jumped, it was as if there were several rattlesnakes under us.

"What—For crying out loud, what?" I yelled, not seeing anything but gray.

"The sidewalk! Look, the sidewalk is here," he said.

"Just where else would it be?" Jake asked, looking to us for answers.

"I don't know," he said, "but my mom said they roll up the sidewalks in this Podunk town at nine o'clock. They must've forgotten to roll them up tonight. Should we call someone?"

We all looked to the others as if to ask if he really was that stupid. Then he bent over and busted out laughing. I think we all felt about the same, wanting to beat the crap out of him for scaring us like he just did. Instead, we just threw our hand in the air and kept walking.

"Let's go get us a ghost," Charlie grinned, heading back towards the river.

When we were out of the streetlights, Charlie and I turned our flashlights on. In my flashlight, the batteries or the connection was bad. It would grow really weak then go out altogether. Once I banged it against my leg, it would come back on as bright as a brand new one for three or four minutes then start fading out again.

"Heck of a nice flashlight," Jake said.

"Yeah, even better than the one you forgot to bring," I said, pointing the newly brightened light in his face to kill his vision.

He put his hand in the way of the light. "I told you my dad has it. He would kill me if he found out I took it."

Getting to the spot Mr. Podolak told us about was not all that easy. We had to slide down a steep bank and wade through some tall sunflowers and a bunch of grass. If I was going to do any kissing on a girl, I think I could have picked a much better spot than this. This place had to have been a lot easier to get to all those years ago. No boy would bring a girl to a place like this.

Shining our lights under the bridge, we saw a bunch of empty bean cans, a few beer bottles, and even two Coke bottles. I made a mental note to come back for them in the daylight and collect the six cents the bottle deposit would bring me.

You could feel the tension between us. We were all scared, but who would be the first to admit it? The joking was gone. We all stayed in more or less a wad. If one guy moved a little this way or that, the others would follow along.

"What time is it?" Gary asked to no one in particular.

Hitting my flashlight against my leg to get it a bit brighter, I shined it on my watch. "I got eight minutes to midnight." I told the others.

"Is that the right time?" Jake asked.

"Well, it's the right time for us, seeing that I am the only one in the bunch with a watch," I said.

"What if that isn't the right time," Charlie chimed in. "What if it is a lot later and she has gone."

"A ghost ain't like no train. They ain't on no time table. It ain't like a ghost will show up at twelve o'clock sharp or two o'clock. They can be anyplace they want as long as it's dark outside and somewhere close to where they was killed," Bruce said.

"Well, where do ghosts go in the daytime?" I asked, genuinely curious.

"I'm not real sure, but I bet the sun makes them dissolve. Then, when darkness comes, they appear again. Not real sure about the dissolves part, but no one in the entire world has ever seen a ghost in the daylight," Bruce continued, though I wasn't too sure about his thinking.

Sitting in a tight group, we decided to turn the flashlights off, sit in the moonlight, and see if anything happened.

If one of us moved, the others would turn to see what the matter was. One time, a stick or piece of weed stuck me in the back. I jumped forward more or less from the tickle; however, you would have thought the devil himself grabbed hold of me from the way the others acted.

Gary jumped up as if he was getting ready to take off in a dead run. Charlie jerked away from me, letting out what I called a little sissy scream. The others just set there in a frozen daze, not knowing what to do. It was the same as that proverbial deer in the headlights. Jake and Bruce both just had blank stares on their faces. I think Fat Lucy who lived across the street from the feed store could have kissed both of them boys square on the mouth. They were frozen in time.

I didn't have any idea what to say to them after causing such a commotion, so I just pulled the little twig from behind me, held it in the air, and said, "Twig."

"God, Sonny, you nearly to scared me to death," Gary said. "I was no more than a half second from crapping my pants. All because of a little old twig? Crap, man, next time something like that pokes, you say something before you jump. Jesus." He plopped back down.

Sitting there in the moonlight would have been a good time to tell ghost stories, but none of us was up for that. It was spooky enough just setting there. We sure didn't need to fuel the fire with any ghost stories.

"Run, Guys! Run for your life! My god, there she is! Run!" Bruce said as he jumped to his feet, pointing toward something coming over the river.

We all jumped to our feet, ready to run for our lives. We were not sure what a ghost could do to a human, but we sure as heck didn't want to be the first to find out.

"Where? Where is she?" Charlie asked in the most frighten voice I had ever heard.

"There, guys! There! Her eyes! Her eyes!" Bruce said, pointing at two lights coming toward us.

I looked for a second, not wanting to be the only one that didn't see her.

"Wait a second. That ain't her. That ain't no ghost you stupid fool. That's nothing but fireflies."

A smile started creeping back onto Bruce's face once he realized it wasn't a killer ghost coming our way.

When we were all again seated, a little smile came to Jake's face then a little smirk. A small laugh crept out that seemed to catch on to the others. In a second or two, a full gut wrenching laugh was coming from all of us. Even Bruce, the one all the laughing was directed at, was doubled up in the dirt.

I don't know if it was all that funny or if it was just to break the nervousness that we seemed to all be feeling.

As the laughter died down, Bruce got real quiet and put his finger to his lips. "Listen," he said.

"What now? Them fireflies flapping their tiny little wings too loud?" Charlie asked, smiling and hoping the others would get the half-hearted joke.

"No. Listen. Hear that?" Bruce said again, listening hard to hear over the trickle of water.

"Crap, that's just your run-of-the-mill howl," I said, hoping that was truly what it was.

As we all listened, there was no mistaking that there was indeed a sound of some kind. It was real faint. You really had to strain to hear it, but the harder we listened, the louder it seemed to get.

"It's a cow, dog, or something like that," Jake said with a look on his face that pleaded for agreement.

"Sure, that's got to be it," I said, trying to build my own courage somewhat. Looking around at the others, I couldn't make out their faces all that well in the moon light. However, the one thing I did see was pure fright - the kind of fright you feel when someone tells you that you are fixing to die the most horrible death in the world.

A couple of them, Charlie and Gary, were on the verge of running. Bruce was in a daze, hand up to his ear, trying to hear whatever it was he was hearing. Anyone could see he was scared out of his mind. The hand he was holding by his ear was shaking like old Mr. Heeths hand, and Mr. Heeths was in the last stage of Parkinson's disease.

Suddenly, the most god awful scream echoed across the stream. It sounded like that girl was getting her head cut off at that very morning.

When we heard that scream, it did it in for all of us. Charlie screamed. He didn't scream anything that you could understand; only screamed. The others were half way up the steep little hill before I could get moving.

I could hear Bruce saying to himself, "Ho, God. Ho, God. Ho, God."

Jake was yelling, "Get out the way," to me over and over in the moonlight.

I could smell something terrible. I could smell it as I ran for my dear life a few steps behind the others. I wasn't sure which one of them had done it, but the smell left no doubt that one of them had crapped in his pants.

No matter who had done the deed, we were all running for all we were worth. If this had been a race, there would have been no one in Verden that could have beaten us that night. I would have gone as far as to say that there was probably no one in the state of Oklahoma that could have held a candle to us.

When we got to the street light in front of the bank, we slowed to a walk. As we were walking along, I could see where Bruce's pants were wet. Charlie had a small damp spot on his jeans as well.

Then I realized the worst smell was not coming from one of them, but from me. It had scared the crap out of me. If the others found this out, I was a goner. I would have had to move to another state, because I would never live that down.

"Let's get the hell out of here," I said. "Who's to know that we are not being followed?"

That was all I had to say. We all took off in a dead run for our prospective homes. I imagined that the others wanted to hide whatever it was they had done to themselves as well as I did.

When I got home, I went straight to the bathroom, cleaned myself up, and went to bed. I didn't even close my eyes that night.

About three weeks after all that happened, we boys were again setting on the bench in front of the store when Mr. Podolak walked up, accompanied by his two granddaughters.

"Hi there, boys. You ever go down to that ol' river to find Donna's ghost?" he asked.

None of us answered him. I guess we just wanted to forget that part of our lives completely. In fact, we'd barely even discussed it amongst ourselves.

"Ho, by the way, boys, these are my granddaughters, Lasie and Lindsey. They're from Mount Holley, here to visit me for a couple of weeks." he said, resting a hand on each girl's shoulder in turn.

"Hi," we all said together.

"By the way, boys, please don't ever scare my girls here, 'cause they scare so easy."

We all looked at him kind of dumfounded, because we didn't even know these Girls. We had no reason to be scaring them.

"Not to worry, we won't," Gary said, turning away as to leave.

"Just making sure," Mr. Podolak said, "because when they get scared, they scream like a couple of scalded hogs." A smile crept onto his face, "Go ahead, girls. Show the boy how you scream."

With that, the two girls let out a couple of screams that made the hair stand up on our necks. Not because they were so loud, but because they were the same screams we had heard at the river.

We could do nothing but look at one another, mouths wide open.

Jake summed it all up with one good sentence, "Well, I'll be a son of a bitch. Don't that just blow your dress up?"

Chapter Nine

One summer evening, I was sitting on the front porch, watching a large black storm cloud moving in from the northeast.

My mother would come out every so often to look up at the clouds. She was deathly afraid of storms. Many a time, she would make me get into the bathtub with her. She'd pull the mattress from her bed over us, hoping that when the house was blown to smithereens, that the bathtub and mattress would protect us.

My grandmother made fun of her all the time. "That old mattress sure ain't going to do you no good. If'n this here house was to get hit by one of them twisters, heck, you wouldn't even be able to hold onto that thing. You and the boy would be carried away only God knows how far or how high," she would say, showing her discolored teeth with a smile.

Being pushed down in some old bathtub was sure not my way of getting out of a tornado. I would much rather just take my chances sitting on the living room couch. At least when it was all over, I would not have to explain to anyone why I was sitting in the middle of town in a bathtub with my mother holding on to some dirty old mattress.

With my luck, I would end up getting blown to Nebraska or Kansas like that Dorothy girl. There wouldn't be that witch there or little people; Munchkins, I think they were called. No, I would end up in the middle of a baseball park or football game with thousands of people staring down at mother and me in that stupid bathtub. Now, how in God's name would a twelve year old boy ever explain that?

Just as long streaks of lighting started flashing across the blackened sky, small drops of rain started hitting on the broken sidewalk running up to our house. I decided that I'd better move my chair a bit back from the edge of the porch if I didn't want to get wet.

As I was moving my chair back, I saw the front door of Mr. Finchmoore's open. He walked to the edge of his porch, first looking up at the large black cloud gathered over head, then over at me. In most cases, I would have waved to a person, but I knew as well as everyone else that Mr. Herman Finchmoore did not say hello, nor was he ever known to wave to anyone.

He had lived next door to my grandmother for what she said was forever. My grandmother said he had lived alone for over thirty-seven years since his wife had left him to go tend to her sick mother in Chicago.

Poor Mr. Finchmoore had to be the only person in Verden that believed that story, because everyone in town knew she had run off with some young guy she met at the store. That man was just hitchhiking through to someplace in Mississippi to work on a shrimp boat. Story goes, Mrs. Finchmoore walked to the store to buy a small box of brown sugar to make a cake. On her way to the store, she met up with the young hitchhiker. They got to walking along, him telling her about all the faraway places he had visited and about his exciting jobs on different boats. Apparently, he made good money in his many jobs.

Seems to me, if he made all that good of money, he wouldn't have been hitching. He would have had money for a car or, at the very least, a Greyhound bus ticket.

Mrs. Finchmoore's must have been a dreamer or must have fallen into whatever spell a person falls into when they think about faraway places. Right there on that very spot, a block away from the store with a small box of brown sugar in her hand, she decided to leave Herman to hitchhike with the boy. He had promised to make her cook on one of the many boats.

When she got home, she told her husband that she had just got word that her mother was in a trolley accident in Chicago, and that she had to leave right away to go tend to her. As grandmother said, he must have been about a half pound short of the brains people need, because Mr. Finchmoore gave her all the money they had hidden in a green bean can.

Her last words to him were, "Honey, keep checking the mail. I will write you often." With that, she walked around the corner, grabbed hold of the boy's hand, and left, heading for God knows where.

Well, to this day Mr. Finchmoore has done just as his wife had asked him. He checked the mail not once a day or twice; he checked it ten maybe twenty times a day.

When he first started checking for a letter from her, it was only once or twice a day. However, as the years went by, his routine increased tenfold.

It got to be a joke, him checking mail at first; but, after a while, it just became a normal thing. When someone saw him walking to the mailbox at five in the morning or ten at night, people just said, "Old Herman is just checking for a letter."

He would check in the middle of the night. He'd check when it was cold or hot outside. It made no matter to him. Checking for a letter from his beloved wife came before anything else.

Mr. Tibbitts, the assistant bank manager, went by one afternoon when he was checking his mail and said he was in the mind to tell him about his wife running off to be a shrimper. When he started talking about her, though, he said he had seen a look in Mr. Finchmoore's eyes that looked to be anger. Well, Mr. Tibbits decided it would probably be better to just let it alone, let the old fool check his mail. In fact, if Herman wanted to pitch a tent by the mail box, it wouldn't have surprised a soul.

You would have thought God himself came down and slapped me across the face when a big old clap of lighting hit, or felt like it hit, nearby. That loud cracking sound next to me darn near made me fall out of my chair.

I looked over at Mr. Finchmoore's house. He was still standing on the porch, looking at me. Then he turned toward his mailbox, walked out slow - being as old as he was-, opened the mailbox, and peered inside. Seeing nothing, he closed it and started his slow walk back to the cover of his front porch back into the house, slamming the door when he reached his haven.

I sat there as the wind whipped around in the trees, watching the heavy rain fall for several minutes. I wasn't thinking about anything in particular; I just found myself enjoying the thunder storm going on around me. Thankfully, my mother had heard that there was no tornado warning for our county. There would be no shame of the bathtub today.

All of a sudden, it started to hail small pea-size stones. After a minute, the hail stones got bigger, up to quarter size hail. Then one of the worst hail storms I had ever seen started. The stones were about the size of eggs.

It sounded like there were a hundred or more men on the roof, beating it with hammers, some hitting the roof while the others hit tin cans they had with them. It was so loud that even my grandmother and mother came out to see what was happening.

"Good gosh almighty, sounds like the devil himself beating on the side of the house. Would you look at the size of them stones," grandmother said, turning to walk back into the house with mother. I saw a little bit of a shake run through her.

I again just leaned back in my chair to watch the storm.

When I saw Mr. Finchmoore's door open again, I figured the hail had also brought him outside to witness the goings-on. When he looked around like he always did, I knew what he had in mind.

Surely not—not in this storm. The hail stones would knock him out or not beat him right to death, I thought to myself.

I didn't know him all that well. In fact, I didn't really know him at all, but I knew enough about him that I didn't want to see him get hurt. Thank god, right after, he turned to back in the house. Rain, sleet, snow, or hail will not stop the mailman, but at least the size of the hail stones would stop Mr. Finchmoore from another trip to his blasted old mailbox.

I breathed a sigh of relief, but it was short lived. In less than two minutes, Mr. Finchmoore shoved open the door again. This time when he stepped outside, he was carrying a pee pot, a five gallon, white porcelain pot. When I saw it, I knew exactly what it was because my granny kept the same one under her bed.

For the life of me, I had no idea why he would be carrying a pee pot around with him, but then people said he was a strange bird anyway. Then I saw him move the empty pot over his head. I had no doubt what he was going to do next. Sure enough, holding the pot a few inches over him, he stepped off his porch and headed toward the mail box. I wanted to laugh or scream at him, "Get back on the porch, you old fool."

I couldn't believe what was taking place before me. As he slowly walked toward the mailbox, the large hail stones would strike the pee pot, knocking little chunks of porcelain off of it leaving little black spots. When the stones hit his back or his legs, I could see him flinch in pain. It hurt me to watch what was happening to him.

When he reached the mailbox, he pulled the small door down, getting hit in the hand at the same time. Jerking his hand away real fast, he bent over to look inside. Seeing nothing of course, he closed the door using his elbow, keeping his sore hand tucked in next to his stomach.

As he headed back to the house, he would jerk this way and that. It was a little like a hop and skip; the best someone in their eighties could do. About five feet from his porch, I saw a big piece hit him square in the middle of his back. He went down to his knees with a thud and a grunt. As I looked around with fear in my heart for something to rescue him with, I saw him crawl back up on the porch with the little energy he had left.

The pot he had left on the ground no longer looked like the pee pot my grandmother had. It looked like some old pot that had been shot several times by a shotgun.

Poor old Mr. Finchmoore just lay there. I knew he wasn't dead because every once in a while he would move his legs. I knew that the old man had to be hurting in the most awful way. That and only that deterred me from running out into the hail myself to go see if he was okay.

When the hail stopped, I debated for a second whether to go get my mother and grandmother or go myself to see if he was okay. Believe me, I had a lot of things I would rather do than go check on some old crabby old man that might chew your head off. I thought, *Okay, I will just watch him for one more minute to see if he gets up.* Then the other side of my mind chimed in, *What if he is hurt and hurt bad, bleeding or something. If I wait, he just might die, bleeding to death or something.* If he died and I watched, could they get me for something? *Good gosh, I wonder if they could get a person for murder if they just watched a guy die and did nothing.*

That made my mind up for me. No matter what could happen, I had to go check on him. If he got mad, that just had to be the way it was. I was sure not going to go to prison for some crabby old man.

Chapter 10

Going over to check on an old man that you weren't sure if he was on his last breath was a weird feeling. I had never seen anyone die before. The closest I ever came to seeing anyone die was when six-year-old Debbie Truss had been standing on the bank, blowing on some dandelions she had found growing near the water. The little seeds must have not been hitting the water like she wanted. The way I saw it, she must've decided to move a little closer to the edge. She stepped on an old five-gallon can someone must have used as a seat way back when. After being in that murky water, the can must not have looked too good to carry back.

It must've been a little slick in the one place without rust, the one piece that she decided to step on. One minute, she was as happy as a kid with a new toy, blowing on the dandelions. The next, she was a little girl in a panic, having fallen face first into the slow-moving river. She threw her arms into the air and kicked like a dying fish, but nothing stopped her from going under.

By the time I got down to where she fell, she had fought and splashed her way several feet from the shore. I looked around for something to hold out to her. Finding nothing, I turned back around, ready to jump in to save her. I guess I must have taken longer than I thought because there were three men in the water trying to find her already. They would surface, take a large lungful of fresh air, then dive back down, feeling around since they couldn't see in the brown, murky water. This seemed to go on for several minutes, but in reality it couldn't have been but a minute or two.

"Here! She's here!" Mr. Warren said, pulling the young girl up by her dirty t-shirt. Several of the men that had been fishing in the area came running to the edge of the water to take the young girl from Mr. Warren.

The man who grabbed her was not a bit gentle about what he was doing. I would have thought he would of at least been easy with the poor drown girl.

I was told later that he was in such a hurry to get air back into the little girl that being gentle was the last thing on his mind.

More or less throwing the girl onto her back, he began forcing air down into the girl's lungs with his own. He continued for several seconds.

I had long given up hope ever seeing her alive after the way she looked being pulled out of the water. You could see from the expressions on the faces of the others standing around that hope had long since gone from them as well.

However, with him still going, I first heard a slight cough. Then she coughed real hard and water sprayed from her mouth. Once it was all out, she started sobbing uncontrollably.

"She's back. She's alive," someone said from the crowd standing around, watching the goings on.

I was excited, even happy, she made it. I had never seen a dead person before. In truth, I wasn't sure if I was all that excited about her living again, or that I could go on living without seeing a dead person.

Chapter 11

Leaning down next to Mr. Finchmoore, I could see his eyes were closed. I knew he was breathing because I could see and hear him taking large breaths.

I didn't want to touch him, but I knew I had to kind of shake him if I were to find out if he was okay. I decided I would give him a little shake, and, if he didn't respond, then I would run get my mother or grandmother.

Placing my hand on his wet shoulder, I gave him a quick shake. Nothing. I wanted to just go get my mother, but I knew I better be sure. All I needed was to run and get her in a panic only to have her find this old man sitting in a chair, bitching at us for being on his porch.

Reaching down, I shook his shoulder again, this time shaking it kind of hard. Before I could remove my hand, his hand came up and clamped down on mine. I nearly peed myself, I got such a fright.

I tried to pull my hand out from under his, but his grasp was way stronger than mine. I instantly understood two things: first, he was going to be okay, and second, I just might be in what my cousin Lisa said, "A nine line bind." Never quite understood what she meant, but that was what I was in. Not good.

I wanted to scream, "Let me go. I only came to help you, you old fool." Instead, I just froze and didn't say a word.

Then he started patting my hand with his. I wasn't sure what he meant by that until he started to sit up and start talking again.

"Thanks, boy. Thanks for trying to help me," he said.

"I... I...," was all I could seem to get out.

When he got to his feet, moved over to an old brown rocker, and sat down, he said, "Hail damned near got me this time. Been through several of them hail storms, but nothing like this one. Course, I wasn't stupid enough to check mail then."

Listening to him talk, he sounded just like any other old man I had been around. I had always thought he was just a crazy old man that checked his mail all day long day in day out.

I wasn't sure how to answer him, so I did just what any other boy my age would have done in my place; I didn't say a word. I just let him do the talking. I didn't want to offend him. Only God knows what he might do.

"Been a longtime since anyone ever came to see me, even if it was just to see if I got my fool self killed by this old storm.

"In fact, I believe you are the first human being who's been on this porch in something like six, eight months. Had a couple of town ladies – ladies, I like to call do-gooders - come to the edge of the porch, trying to get me to come out so they could Bible preach to me. Never paid them much mind. Fact is, they could stand there preaching the Bible to me for a month, and they would never change a hair on me.

"Can't stand me them good-for-nothing do-gooders, talkin' that bible stuff in broad daylight. Then, when it gets dark outside, they are more than likely at some bar, half drunk and trying to get picked up by some perverted guy. You can bet your last dollar that they ain't going home to do no explaining how Noah got that boat of his water like he did. No sir, them Bible packing ladies ain't packing no bible after dark.

"Boy, you want something to drink?" he asked, looking down at me half-sitting, half-kneeling by his old rocker.

I shook my head no.

"Well, I sure enough do," he said, getting out of the chair with more grace than I thought an old man his age should have, especially an old man that just got beat to a pulp in a hail storm.

He disappeared behind his screen door into the darkness. I knew this was a chance for me to beat feet out of there, but, for some unknown reason, this old man kind of intrigued me. If nothing else, it was kind of funny the way he explained things.

In less than a minute, he was pushing the screen open again He handed me a cup of hot coffee before taking his seat in the old rocker again.

"Drink it while it's hot," he said, looking into his own cup.

I'd never had coffee before. Always thought is smelled good cooking on the stove, but it just was something that was never brought to me. In the morning, I would either have a glass of milk or orange juice with my breakfast. Grandmother, on the other hand always said, "Boy, don't talk to me – heck, boy, don't even look at me - until I have my morning coffee.

I tried to take a sip, but it was just too hot for me. Taking the little spoon that was in it, I started stirring the stuff, hoping to cool it off. I knew this was what the spoon was for by watching my mother and grandmother over the years.

As I was stirring the coffee, Mr. Finchmoore leaned over to place his saucer and cup on the porch floor. He stood up and started toward the mailbox. I didn't even have to think about what he was doing. He was on his way to the old mailbox again after almost being killed.

Watching him walking toward the mailbox, I felt it was time for me to leave. However, this old man didn't seem a threat to me, so my curiosity wouldn't let me leave.

On his way back from the box, I could see a slight smile slip onto his face. It began at each corner of his mouth, and, by the time he placed his first foot on the steps, his grin had turned into a smile that covered his face.

Sitting back down and picking up his coffee, he began to talk and snicker at the same time. "These old bats around here think I'm as crazy as a loon checking my mail every few minutes. They think my wife took off with another man, and that drove me over the brink to Nutsville or Bedbugville if there is such a place. Believe me; I hear it when people say he is nuttier than a bag full of bedbugs.

"Bag full of bed bugs, crap, that is nuts itself. Who ever heard of a bag full of bedbugs," he said, taking a snickering sip of coffee.

"The truth is I know she left with another man. She left me high and dry, but that was about the best thing that ever happened to me. When I was a kid, I thought seeing a naked girl was about the only thing I had to live for. Nope, getting rid of my wife has to be the highlight of my life," he said, placing his cup on the floor so he could lean back and get comfortable.

I was confused by then because, as long as I could remember, the story was he was heartbroken over her leaving him. All the poor man could do was check the mail over and over, hoping she was coming home.

"She couldn't cook. I lost my dog because of her cooking. Well, I guess a little of that was my fault. She made me a hamburger steak with brown gravy, and, I swear to God, that piece of meat had to be the worst tasting piece of crap a grown man ever put between his teeth. It was so bad that I couldn't throw up. I was afraid if I threw up the taste, the second time would plum kill me. Instead, I fed it to my dog, Tuffy. I guess I named him wrong when I called him Tuffy because, when he woofed it down, he gave me one look and ran outside. Before he could get to the gate, he started shaking like all get out and fell over dead. Now, he didn't fall over and have a hard time breathing or try to get up. Nope, that dog fell over dead. He was so dead, I ain't sure that rigor mortis hadn't done set in before he hit the ground.

"And pass gas, I'll tell you kid," then kind of froze in place like he forgot something. "By the way, boy, I ain't a bit sure I even know your name."

"Sonny," I said, placing my cup next to his, hoping he would go on with the story.

"Like I was saying, Sonny, this woman could pass just some of that gas. It was like someone had knocked off that little valve on the propane tank and let all the propane out in one big blast. I know you won't believe this at all, but the blanket on our bed would flutter like someone was trying to kick it off for dear life. It scared me the first time it happened. I was standing there admiring how pretty she was sleeping. All of a damned sudden, the bed sheet went flying up a foot, maybe even two feet, in the air. That God awful farting sound came out from under that sheet and scared the crap out of me. I tell you, Boy, I thought the devil himself was under that sheet, trying to get me by the throat.

"I was sure I had gone and married a girl that was possessed by the devil himself. If not the devil himself, it had to be one of his demons for sure. I was ready to beat it out of that room – heck, out of the house. I hate to say it like this to a boy as young as you, but I was plum scared shitless.

"Then the smell started coming out from under that blanket. It wasn't a smell that kind of got to you. No, that smell took complete control of you all at once. I guess it might be like being shot. Once the bullet hits, the damage is done before you even know you have been shot."

"Same about that smell she put out. One second you smell normal smells around you, then, all of a sudden, you are looking for a place to throw up."

He had me hanging on every word. I didn't think he was nuts at all by the way he talked.

"And stink. I tell you, boy, that woman could stink up a house. She made the paint on our bedroom walls curl up and turn yellow - as yellow as one of them little Jap guys our boys just got through fighting over there in the war."

"And another thing," he said, leaning over close to me. "I don't 'spect you to be telling anyone this story, now, boy."

I just shook my head no. I guess that was enough for him because he leaned back in the old rocker and started talking again.

"I'm not real sure about this," he started again. "You never saw nobody walk by our house. I believe the word got out quick after a few people got themselves a good whiff of the smell coming from the house. Just thank the good lord up there that no one ever died with a heart attack after walking unknown into the stink cloud.

"Sure, these people think I'm plum heartbroken over that woman leaving. They got it into their heads that I pine away in the house here all day, checking the mail in hopes that a letter may show up.

"The truth is, I wouldn't take that woman back if God himself came down here, set beside you and me, right here on this porch, and said, 'Finchmoore, now look here. I want you to take your wife back.' 'Nope,' I would just have to say. "Lord, I can't. She done cheated on me and, for your sake," wouldn't want to say for God's sake with him sitting right here among us you know, 'I hope you don't make me.'"

With that, he got up, picked up the two cups, and walked back into the house. I didn't know if I should sit there waiting for him to come back or just go home.

As I got up to leave, his door opened. "Where you off to boy?"

"Stretching my legs," was all I could come up with in such a short notice.

Walking over by me, he said, "I hope you don't give me away. I'm getting old now. Heck, I might as well face the truth. I am old now. Watching peoples' faces when I make one of them stupid trips to the mailbox is about all I have left in this old world.

"Tell you what, boy. Bring your friends over tomorrow, and we can all have a little fun," he said, turning to walk back into the house.

After all this time, these years, I had believed that he was just a nutso old man living next door to my grandmother. Now finding out that he was just as sane as anyone living in Verden was about the biggest surprise I had that summer. I couldn't wait to tell the guys, see if they believed it. It was hard to change one's mind after they've been thinking something for so long. Heck, I wasn't even sure if I believed my own mind.

R.J. BURROUGHS

Chapter 12

I spent a lot of my extra time with Mr. Finchmoore after that. When I wasn't running with my friends or getting in trouble with my grandmother, I would sit on his front pouch with him talking about the old days.

He loved telling stories about way back when. He always started a new story with, "Way back when." When I heard that, I knew it was time to hunker down for one of his long winded stories. Believe me; some of them were long winded. I had to eat a cold supper more times than I could count because of one of his way back when stories.

I had no clue whether or not any of them were true because he could tell some real good stories. He could make the hair on the back of your neck not just stand up, but curl up as well.

One evening, we were setting on the porch when, out of nowhere, he got a smile on his face and a tear running from his left eye at the same time. For the life of me, I can't remember doing something like that. Sure, I have laughed so hard that I cried, but never have I, nor have I seen, a man all of a sudden get a big old smile and tears.

I asked him, "Mr. Finchmoore, are you okay?"

Looking down at me, he said, "Yes, boy. I guess I am just missing old Tucker that's about all."

I knew, just as sure as the world was round and that it was near impossible to push over a cow, I should not ask who Tucker was. I knew he was setting me up, wanting me to ask, but this time I wasn't about to bite. Not this time when mother was fixing chicken fried steak for supper. That was my all-time very favorite meal, and I sure didn't want to sit down to it cold.

I could see him eyeing me, looking down ever so slightly, and hoping curiosity would get the better of me. I just looked over toward my own home, hoping he would change his mind and start talking about something else.

He was having no part of that. He was going to tell me this story if it was the last thing he ever did in this old world.

"You ever have a Tucker in your life, Boy," he asked.

"No, sir, can't say as I have," I said, still looking off into the distance.

I knew he almost had me. I came close as the hair on a fly's back to asking, "Who is Tucker," but I didn't. He knew I was doing all in my power to not ask, but he was as determined to get me to ask as I was not to. Then he had me before I even knew I was had. He lowered his head and whimpered a little to himself. I thought he was darn near going to bust out in tears any second.

"Who was Tucker?" I asked.

In an instant, his mouth started turning from a frown into a smile so wide I thought the corners of his mouth might tear a little bit.

"Let me tell you this boy. Tucker was one fine rooster, and big. That rooster was nearly as big as a German Shepherd. 'Course, that may be a little of exaggeration on my part, but that chicken was a big one. Many was the time I saw him chase dogs, cats, and even people out of this yard right here," he said, pointing to his overgrown lawn.

Gosh, I wanted to eat my chicken fried steak warm, but I knew in my heart, that was not to be. By the time he was through bragging on his chicken, my dinner would be cold. Not even a bit warm, just plain old cold.

"One day, I saw Tucker chase a full grown - I'm talking a full grown, mind you - Chinaman out of that there yard right there," he said, moving his finger back and forth to cover the complete yard.

"I never did find out for sure what that Chinaman wanted coming up here. Anyways, Mrs. Glister, who used to live across town, said he was selling a wok. I guess he could have been selling a wok. I'm not all too sure. Heck, I ain't even sure what a wok is.

"Anyways, Mrs. Glister said she was walking by my place when this Chinese fellow comes running out the gate, screaming something awful. She had no idea what he was screaming about since she didn't talk no Chinaman, but she said it scared her something awful," he said, snickering.

"I bet you this, Sonny Boy, if she had any of them adult diapers you see advertised on TV day in and day out, she would have used hers up in one lickety-split. She said she saw that Chinese fellow screaming, running from my yard with that big old red and white rooster following behind.

"She told me that Tucker chased that fellow all the way across the road over yonder, up that hill, and across the railroad tracks. Now I have seen a lot of things in my life, but never nothing like that."

"Anyways, Tucker turned out to be better than any old watch dog. He didn't only keep unwanted riff raff out of my yard, but bugs as well. You know how Chickens like to peck around for bugs, and, as bit as Tucker was, he could eat a lot of bugs."

"The only problem was my wife lived here in those days. I don't think she disliked Tucker all that much; however, I wouldn't go so far as to say she liked him. Back in those days, she and I didn't get along all that well. Heck, to make a long story short, we didn't get along at all. Last nice thing she ever said to me was 'Would you please bring me some toilet paper?'

"I guess I should have taken her that paper, but then that's another story," he said, looking somewhere in the distance.

That night, I lay in bed thinking about Mr. Finchmoore. After you got to know him, he was a likeable enough fellow. All the problems he's had in his life, it's no wonder he didn't want anything to do with people, his wife leaving him like she did, the towns people thinking he was a nut. It felt kind of good to be in his life, bringing what joy I could to the old man.

Wouldn't it be great if we could get back at his wife for the way she had treated him. I knew that was impossible, not knowing where she was or if she was even alive these days. I had no idea how to get back at the town for the way they had shunned him. There must have been some way.

I did, however, come up with a plan to at least get the guys and scare the crap out of them. Laying there, thinking about what I could do with Mr. Finchmoore's help, kept me awake way into the morning hours. By the time I drifted off to sleep, I had concocted a plan that would be the mother of all plans.

Chapter 13

That next evening, I was sitting on the porch with Mr. Finchmoore. We weren't doing much other than talking about a few of the townspeople, likes and dislikes. I decided to hit the subject right there and then.

"Mr. Finchmoore,' I started, "we've become pretty good friends over the last few weeks, haven't we?" I wasn't looking him in the eyes like I had always done. It was, I guess, the fear he might say, "No".

The answer was hardly one that I had expected. He didn't only say that we, sure enough, had become good friends; he even went as far to say that we were buddies.

"Well then, Mr. Finchmoore, - I mean buddy - if I had a way to pull a prank on my friends, is there a chance you might help me?" I pulled the same trick again, staring at the porch. This was a much different kind of question.

"Well, I see no reasons why I shouldn't help you as long as there isn't a chance someone might get himself killed or hurt bad. What I mean is, if there is some blood or bleeding involved in this here prank, I'm not sure if I can oblige you," he said, raising an eyebrow over to me.

Now that I had his answer, now that I knew he would help me, I looked him straight in the eyes and started to explain to him what I had in mind. First thing I did was assure him I meant there to be no blood.

I started with the most risky part of the plan. I told him that the first step would be to tell the guys that the old man had a bad heart attack and passed on. That and, since I was his only friend in the entire world, he left everything in his house to me.

As I was telling him about the plan I had come up with, I couldn't help but snicker a bit to myself. A couple of times he even laughed out loud and slapped his leg. I could tell he was all for it immediately. We finished off the day with him telling a couple stories of his own pranks.

Over the next few days, we started the beginning steps. I had him write up a legal looking piece of paper with a bunch of who-fors, thous, haves and have-nots, and even a couple of habeas corpus's thrown in for good measure - whatever a habeas corpus might be.

He said that his plan was to not show himself for a couple of days. When the guys asked later on where he was, I would say he'd died and his kin came picked up his body, taking him back to Arkansas or someplace to bury him. Then, I would tell them that a lawyer from Oklahoma City brought me the document saying that he had left everything in the house to me. It had to be a lawyer from Oklahoma City since we didn't have any lawyers in our small town. Besides, I thought a lawyer from a big city like Oklahoma City had to make it sound more official.

Chapter 14

Of course, me being curious as I was to make it all official, I had asked my grandmother that week, "Why no lawyer in Verden?" I'd never had a reason to ask before.

My grandmother had said, "We had a lawyer once in Verden. He nearly starved to death trying to drum up business in town. I guess there never was any legal stuff around. There wasn't much in the way of divorce back in those days. I guess men and women just naturally got along better before TV since they had to set around and talk.

"There were a lot of chicken thieves back then, but that was taken care of mostly by rock salt from a farmer's shot gun. A load of rock salt in the old behind usually cured a guy from thieving chickens.

"Last time this town needed a lawyer was way back when."

She liked to use way back when anytime something happened where she couldn't remember the date or if it happened before she was born.

"Way back when, there were a couple of men from someplace far off, like Texas or Kansas. It didn't matter, anyway, where they was from. What mattered most was that they'd got caught stealing a horse, cow, and six watermelons from the Sim's place, six and a half miles east of town.

"The law caught up with them while they were trying to swim them critters across the river. Never did find them watermelons. Townsfolk thought they must have stashed them away, planning to get them animals taken care of and then come back for the melons later.

"Myself, I don't think they took no melons at all. That old Mr. Sim's fellow would soon lie as tell the truth. I remember that, as a little girl, people around here talked about the gosh-awful way he'd lie all the time.

"Why heck," she said, "he was in town once, hanging around and talking to the no accounts like he always did. All those men should have been home working, not jawing on the street corner. Anyways, he was telling them about a skeeter problem he was having out to his place. He said that the 'moskeeters' were something fierce around there, saying they were so big that they could near stand toe to toe with his rooster. When he tried to sleep at night, it sounded like a small airport if a couple of them happened to collide while flying. He kept on going, saying it sounded like one of them cherry bomb firecrackers the kids like to play with. If one of them ever stuck one of their stingers in you, it could near get a pint of blood for you could swat it off.

"He said, the only thing he could do was to catch a couple of the bigger ones and keep them in a gallon jar, feeding them at same time each day. Over a couple of weeks, he was certain he'd made pets out of them two skeeters.

"The finally to his farfetched story was when he said that, when he unscrewed the lid of that jar, first thing they did was fly up and land on his shoulder like a parrot. From that day on, he'd said, his two skeeters, which he named Clem and Clemet cause he couldn't tell if they was boy or girl skeeters, would drive all the other 'moskeeters' out of the house. After then, he slept like a baby, knowing Clem and Clemet was watching over him."

I tapped on the table. She had started staring into her can of snuff. That was my sign that she had completely lost where she was going and what I had asked in the beginning. "Umm... lawyer, grandma?"

She snapped back in and spat some chew out, "Oh yeah... Well, anyone with his right mind - for that matter, half a mind - had to know he was a lying fool. There is no taming 'moskeeters.' A 'moskeeter' don't even have a brain to teach. That lying old fool.

"Anyways, back to those two guys that stole the horse and cow. They didn't put up no fight when the law caught them and took them back to that little jail we have at the end of town.

"They were locked up there for five or six days, waiting for a judge to come up from Okie City to try them. When the trial was all done, them two got six months in jail. Guess they didn't figure they could do no six months in that little jail, 'cause, when the first opportunity struck, they broke jail and ran, stealing an old thirty-two Ford Coupe. They were beating feet out of town when Mr. Overmire stepped off the curb in front them two fleeing crooks. Without as much as by-your-leave or kiss-my-backside, they ran smooth over him."

"Tell you what, when a thirty-two Ford hits you broadside, going full out, it is a wonder you ain't dead before you hit the ground. Well, as luck had it, that old Mr. Overmire was a World War II war veteran. He got his two legs blown off at Saipan, so, when that Ford hit him, all it did was destroy his legs that were made of no more than toothpicks. All that happened to him was, when he got tossed over the car, he landed on his back side around back of the car."

"Well, when the law caught up with them two boys, they needed a lawyer. They near got life in state prison, which they should have gotten anyway - as much meanness as them two was up to. However, they got a lawyer from the city that got them off with one year in state prison, and they weren't allowed to come back to this town for the rest of their lives."

"It was that day that we learned that our town lawyer wasn't much good at the law. In such a small town, it wasn't hard to get the word around. No one gave him anymore business, and he flew out almost as fast as the men from that there jail."

Chapter 15

Two weeks before we boys had to go back to school, Mr. Finchmoore and I put our plan into action. It had been at least a week since anyone had seen Mr. Finchmoore, just as we had planned. For the life of me, I couldn't understand why no one had asked about him, especially Gary. Gary was the type person that wanted to know what was going on at all times.

At about two p.m. on a Friday afternoon, finally, Charlie asked about him. "Has anyone seen or talked to old Mr. Finchmoore?" he asked.

Charlie called anyone that was older than he was, "old man" or "old woman." They didn't have to be much older than him either. He once called a girl who had just graduated from school the year before an old girl. Myself, I believe that his calling someone old made him feel that much more like a man. Why, I had no idea? I just felt that way.

Either way, I knew this was my chance. This was exactly what I had been waiting for the last few days. "Well guys, I didn't want to tell you this, but I guess it's my place since I was his only real friend," I said to them, trying to look as sad as I could muster. "You guys really didn't hear about Mr. Finchmoore? You mean, your folks didn't say anything about what happened?" I asked switching to a what-the-hell-is-wrong-with-you-people look.

"What happened? Did he find some woman and run down to Mexico to marry up with her?" Gary asked looking to us all with a cackle and a joker's face. Getting his wanted laughter, he continued, "No, I bet he found out where his wife ran off to and went skedaddling after her."

"Bullcrap," Bruce started in. "You fellows know he was mad as all-get-out over what she had done. You can bet your last buck - if you guys had a last buck to bet that is - that he could care less if'n he ever seen that wife of his. I bet he wouldn't even walk across the street to say hi to her if she was right here in Verden. Nope, I bet someone in his family is either darn well sick, about to die, or has kicked the bucket. He is probably just on his way to say his condolences." The smile he flashed up to us showed that he was feeling like he had just solved the one mystery that Sherlock Holmes himself couldn't figure out.

"Well, that is pretty much the truth there, Bruce," I said, looking at him then the others in turn to keep a feeling of suspense.

"I knew it. I just knew it. Something just told me it was someone in his family that was sickly or dead," he said.

"Dead," I answered, keeping it simple.

"Who? Who died?" they all popped out around the same time.

I wanted to play this up as much as I could. It was an important ritual for each of us to make a big to nothing deal over a little something that didn't amount to much.

One time, Charlie's little sister stabbed him in the arm with a small, toy bayonet someone had given him for his birthday, Christmas, or some other occasion. "It didn't matter what occasion it was, just as long as I got it," he had said to me.

The cut on his arm was about as long as the tip of you little finger; it barely broke the skin. If the truth were known, there wasn't even any blood from the scratch, but, by the time he finished telling the story, you would have thought he had landed on the beaches of Saipan with a Marine division.

When the story got to me, the cut was all the way down his arm, straight down to the bone. In fact, the bone was sticking out of his skin in several places, and he had lost somewhere between two to ten gallons of blood.

Hearing how bad he was, I ran to his house, hoping to say goodbye to him before the ambulance or the hearse was there to carry him away.

When I got there almost completely out of breath, thinking I was about to see my best friends body for the last time, you can imagine what I thought when I saw him sitting on the porch with his sister, eating a couple of cold pancakes that had been left over from breakfast.

"Want a pancake?" he asked me, telling his sister to run inside and get me one.

All I could say was, "A pancake? Do I want a pancake? Heck no, I don't want a pancake. I want to see this slash on your arm that is about to take your life. Tommy Fossum told me about it."

"Ho? That," he said, pulling the sleeve up on his white t-shirt.

"I can't believe this crap. Why, that can't even be call a scratch it is so small," I said to him. He told me after that my face was contorted into some weird mixture of relief and anger, having seen the tiny mark.

"Well, it looks a lot better now that it has started to heal. It looked bad when it first happened. Fact is, I thought I was a goner," he said, looking stone serious.

"A goner? That scratch - and I have to stretch the truth a wholesome lot to even call it a scratch - wouldn't cause a least little bit of a problem if it happened to one of them red ants down there," I said, pointing to a bunch of ants that were trying to carry off a piece of pancake that someone had tossed on the cracked and broken sidewalk.

"That's plenty easy for you to say, you not being the one wounded," he said, taking a large size bite out of the pancake.

"Who died?" Gary said to me. The urgency in his voice sounded like he was about to soil himself in anticipation.

"You ain't going to believe this," I said, acting my sad role again, "but Mr. Finchmoore passed away a couple of days ago."

"That's bull crap. He wasn't sick," Charlie said with a half-smile. I think he wanted it to be bull crap, because, in the short time Charlie had known the man, he had grown a real attachment to him. Maybe Mr. Finchmoore had taken the place of the grandparent Charlie had always longed to have.

"No lie?" Bruce asked.

I never understood why any of us said, "No lie." We always lied to each other. It was kind of a sport to us. I guess it just came natural for boys our age to stretch the truth, making things sound much better than they really were. However, my grandmother said that stretching the truth was nothing more than a bald-faced lie. No matter the fun, it was still something that would send us straight to the pit of hell with no stopping for ice cream on our way to damnation. Never did heed much to that one.

"No lie. Mother said that he slipped away most peacefully in his sleep. She said he died of a heart attack or a fast-acting cancer. It could have been the weaker workings of his soul," I said, reciting the lines I had prepared much before. I had tried my best to come up with something that sounded quick and fatal. Weaker working meant nothing to me. It was a phrase I thought I heard my mother talking about once. Something like, "That old woman's bladder was getting weaker and not working," or something like that. It sounded good, so I just threw it in for show.

"Man, that's a shame, a pure shame. I really was getting to like that old man," Bruce said.

"Well, if you ain't lying to us, I hate it a lot myself. He was kind of an old, funny bird. I like old, funny guys. There just ain't enough old, funny guys in the world. There's only old, boring ones," Charlie said.

As if Charlie had lived long enough to know anything about old funny guys, I thought to myself.

"I know, guys," I started, "but you know the kicker to him passing on? He left everything in his house to me."

"To you? Bullcrap. Why would he do that?" Jake asked.

"Don't have a clue, not a clue at all," I said, acting the confused part of my script now.

"Well, it seems to me his wife should be the one that gets everything, not some kid that lived next door to him," Bruce said with a tone of jealousy that I caught, and I tried not to smile.

"Well, when mother told me he left his stuff to me, you could have yanked on my wiener as hard as you liked and I wouldn't have felt a thing. I was too stunned, mind you," I said.

There was a pause before Bruce chimed in, "I've heard stories about old guys like him leaving hundreds of millions of dollars in their mattresses or behind some hidden door." I saw a glint in his eye that reminded me of the pirate books I had read some time ago.

"Mother said that the paper work would be done around 7 p.m. tonight. After that, it will be legal for me to go over to his house and look at his stuff." I said back to Bruce, getting a reply around me of agreement and wide smiles.

"His stuff, my foot, It's your stuff, boy." Jake said.

"Well, it will be as of seven tonight," I answered.

"Can we come with you? Heck, by all rights some of that stuff should be ours as he was our friend as well as yours," Gary asked, but I could tell it was more of a demand.

I looked at them one at a time, then to the clear sky. I acted as if I was kind of studying what Gary just asked. I knew what I was going to tell them, but I wanted them to suffer a little bit. No, I wanted them to suffer a lot; because I was enjoying this way more than any of them could ever know.

"Gosh, I don't know guys," I said.

"Come on, man. We have been through a lot together. A lot, a lot," Charlie said.

"Yeah, think of all the stuff we have done together. Why should this be any different?" Jake said, poking me in the shoulder.

"Besides, if there are millions of dollars stuck in a jar, mattress, or behind some hidden door, we could help you find it. By yourself it would take you a zillion years to spend that much money anyway," Charlie said, poking me as well.

In a couple seconds, I was being prodded on all sides, giving me a reason to unleash the huge smile I had been hiding.

"Okay, but here's the deal. We can't take anything out of the house tonight. You can just claim what you want. When the lawyer tells me what we can take, then whatever you guys have claimed, you can come and get it," I said, looking at each one of them. They were almost salivating at the thought. I don't know why though. We had been in there, and I am sure Mr. Finchmoore wasn't hiding anything. Plus the place smelled a little funny.

"Deal," Jake said, while all of them nodded their heads.

Chapter 16

I could almost see what was going on in each of their minds. Charlie talked about going to far-away places ever since I had known him. Of course that was all of his life since I was three months older than he was. Being only three months older than another baby didn't count for all that much, though. I guess you could have laid the two of us together in the same crib and we would have never have known the difference. That's been my thoughts ever since I started having thoughts. All babies ever do is eat, cry, sleep, cry, use the bathroom in their pants, and cry.

So, no, three months wasn't all that much. I did know Charlie wanted to travel so he had to be thinking of finding some riches and doing just that, just traveling to different countries forever.

Jake wasn't that easy to read. Fact being, Jake was about as easy to read as some little Jap guy you just met. I never knew what was going on in his mind for sure. I only understood there was something going on there not most of the time but all the time.

I was talking to Charlie one evening when Jake walked up to the porch we were sitting on. He didn't say "hi" or "bye," or "Go kiss a possums butt." He just sat down, looked across the way at the train depot for a couple of seconds, got up, and just moseyed on off.

Neither Charlie nor I had an idea what was going on with him that day. After a while, I started to believe that he did all that on purpose. I think he wanted to confuse us. I will give him this: if that was what he had in mind to do, he did a fine job of it. To this day, I am still not sure what was going on in his mind.

The other two, Gary and Bruce didn't give a care what they found in Mr. Finchmoore's house as long as it could be sold somewhere. Those two were money hungry. Every time we guys would chip in to get something like a new baseball, basketball, or a bat, seems the two of them always came up with some stupid excuse why they could only give so little.

We were going to try to buy a new bat once. Charlie had broken our only one trying to chase down a rat that had scared the hebe jeebies out of him when he had walked up to the plate. He screamed like a girl, not a little girl, but a full grown high school girl.

Everyone playing that day hit the ground laughing at him. I guess he thought, to save face, he would chase the critter down and beat the living crap out of it to keep from looking so stupid, however at that point there was absolutely nothing he could have done to better his situation.

This had to have gone on for several minutes before the rat wised up and headed for the trees along the north side of the ball park. Just as the mouse was running out of strength, Charlie raised the bat over his head, bringing it down as hard as he could. He didn't hit that stupid rat though but a low lying branch, breaking the bat smooth in half.

Realizing what he had just done, he turned to face the crowd who were still laughing. We kept on laughing with a renewed strength after seeing him break that bat. He just stood there looking dumb. The more people laughing, the dumber he looked until a slight smile started at each corner of his mouth, turning into a big old dumb smile as big as you please.

Chapter 17

That evening, we boys met on my front porch, waiting for seven o'clock to come. It was as if we were getting ready to go into major combat or at least a big ball game. That was the feeling at least with us all as fidgety as we were and the talk going around.

Charlie was telling Bruce about all the money we would be finding in the walls, his mattress, or some dusty coffee pot stuffed back in some cabinet. He kept going on about a secret door too that would confuse anyone that might happen to see it walking by. Every time he went on about it, I had to stifle a laugh.

Charlie and Bruce, in their minds, would have enough money to buy about anything that was for sale in Oklahoma or Kansas with Texas thrown in to boot.

At seven, I told them I would be right back as I stood up, opening the door to my house. I had to play this thing up to the hilt if I wanted it to go over as I hoped and planned.

I stood in the living room, looking out at the guys sitting over on the porch. Believe me; they were ready to find the riches of the world next door.

Walking back out, I said to them, "Five more minutes, guys, and it is all ours."

I had to play this up big. I had been working on this for several days, and I wanted nothing to go wrong now. If all went as I expected, we would be talking about this for years to come. Just as the last little bit of sunlight was moving across the top of the depot, I knew it was time. I turned our porch light on as pre-planned and stepped onto the porch.

"Okay, guys, this is it. Keep your fingers crossed that there is some good stuff in there," I said to the group looking up at me.

"Yes. Let's do this. Let's do it," Gary said, his voice overflowing with excitement.

They seemed to all rise together. The looks on the guys' faces were looks that I hadn't seen before or, at least, I never thought I had seen before.

If I had to describe what I was seeing in their faces, it would be nothing - nothing at all. They had more of blank stares than sheer wonderment. Their faces showed no emotions at all, but I would hate to think what was going through their minds.

I was sure it was something about the vast riches that were only a few yards - a few steps - away from them. You would have thought they'd have taken off in a dead run, but that wasn't the case at all. In fact, all of them stayed right behind me. As I reached the front porch and reached for the knob, I looked back and the others didn't so much as look at me but at my hand on the knob. I gave it a slow turn and, I couldn't believe it, their eyes stayed with my hand the whole way to the end.

I pushed the door open ever so slightly. We, as a group, peered into the front room. As we looked in, the little light that was in the room was fading fast as night approached. Pushing the door open completely, I reached for the light switch, clicking it up to turn the overhead light on.

"Nothing," I said just loud enough for the others to hear.

"Oh man. Crap. Ho, crap, crap, crap, and triple crap," Jake said, looking at each one of us.

"Well, we got to do this anyway, light or no light," Gary said, kind of pushing his way past the others and me.

"You ever been in here before?" Jake asked me.

"Nope, only on the porch with him," I lied.

"Should we stick together or go our separate ways looking for stuff?" Gary asked no one in particular.

"Let's stick together, guys, like the Musketeers did. Whatever we find that is worth a lot, we will be splitting it anyway," I said, looking toward what I knew was the master bedroom. I guess it was the master, anyway. The house only had two bedrooms and this was the one he slept in.

"Yeah, okay. Sure," were the sounds I got back from them.

The light was darker now than bright as the sun was completely down behind the trees in the front yard. The moon had not even thought about appearing as yet.

I lead them to the bedroom and pushed open the door. Each boy sort of pushed his own way into the room, kind of like each one of us wanted to be first in. Yet, in our hearts, I'm not sure we were quite aware if we would rather be the last or first ones in. A person, or at least a person of twelve years old, walking around in the house of a man we didn't know all that well anyway and had just died was not first on our to do list.

Jake saw Charlie in the large mirror over the dresser drawers. He didn't squeal like a girl, but he did lose his breath to a nice sized gasp.

"You okay?" I asked him. "Sure, just my asthma bothering me a little," he answered.

His asthma? I thought. He had asthma about as much as I had it. His asthma was nothing more than him seeing Charlie in the mirror and catching a bad case of the willies.

The willies were a quick dose of fright. You're not scared enough to wet your pants like you might be when a crazed killer with a large knife is coming at you. It's not enough either to scare you enough to scream like a little girl like when you sneak up behind a person and holler, "Boo." No, the willies are just frightening enough that the hair stands up on the back of your neck. You blow air out of your mouth, but catch yourself before you scream.

I had to kind of giggle to myself—if the image of Charlie in the mirror scared Jake, then what was about to happen would surely cause him to have a barn-burning heart attack.

Pulling the large top drawer out of the dresser, I said, "Good Gosh all Mighty." Those words spoken were as good as a siren.

"What is it? What you find in there, Sonny? Money? Gold? Diamonds? What?" I'm not sure who even asked the question. It seemed to come from all around me at the same time.

"Ah, never mind. It's just a dollar." I said. They sighed together. All their hopes up for nothing, they probably thought. For me, it was all part of the plan.

They were all looking into the drawer when I, in my best acting since I can't remember, turned, dropped the dollar I was holding, and stood straight up, freezing in that position. I stared as hard as I could towards the back wall.

Charlie was first to notice me if there was a first. They all seemed to pick up on it about the same time. Turning to see what I was looking at in such a manner, Charlie let out a little screech that seemed to gain in both momentum and sound as it came out of his mouth.

There, standing against the white wall, was Mr. Finchmoore wearing a white cotton gown that I was sure belonged to his long gone wife. He was completely white from the head, down. I knew it was the flour he had pored over his head to make him look that way, but believe me the others didn't know.

Bruce went straight through the willies, into the screams, and, to what I believe was, the wets as Mr. Finchmoore started slowly moving his arms up from his sides.

The other boys were frozen in place Bruce's screams seemed to not faze them at all. They just seemed frozen like that bronze statue of Clarence Hendrix that stood in front of what once was the drugstore before it went out of business. No one really knew who she was, and I was one of them. Whoever she was, the boys would have made perfect additions to her place in Verden.

When Mr. Finchmoore raised his arms upward, flour dropped off each arm in little puffs. His eyes starting to open very slowly and he started to moan, just a little at first then growing louder and louder.

That was all it took. We were no longer the Musketeers. It was every man for himself. I had never heard sounds like those coming from my friends and I didn't blame them. If I hadn't known, I would have wet myself too due to Mr. Finchmoore's acting and general scariness. I could barely make out one person from the other from the sheer volume of them all put together.

Bruce was screaming like the devil himself was hanging onto the poor boy. Charlie was not making a sound other than the gurgling sounds made by a man in a pure panic, trying to escape the jaws of death. Gary was saying something as he spun towards the nearest exit. I'm sure he was calling for his mommy. I probably couldn't prove that or would I want to, but I would go to my grave with a smile, having that word, "Mommy," in the back of my mind.

It was less than five seconds before I was standing alone in the house with Mr. Finchmoore. I was sure he was going to have to call an ambulance for me, because I could not, as hard as I tried, to stop laughing. However, I'm sure Mr. Finchmoore was in no shape to call anyone for his laughing as well.

I literally fell on the floor while laughing at the guys. What seemed like hours had to be no more than a couple of minutes. Wiping the tears away from laughing so hard, I stood up and headed for the door, wanting to see what happened to my friends.

Walking out onto the porch, I could see there was no one in sight. As dark as it was getting, I was sure they were hiding somewhere close by. Calling out there names, "Charlie, Bruce,

Jake, Gary," I got nothing. I called out to them several times; however, there was only the echo of my own voice in the darkness.

Chapter 18

The next day, meeting the other boys up in town, I told them all about Mr. Finchmoore and I, and we had set them up. I told them how I had gone over earlier to help pour the flour over his head and take the bulb out of the overhead light in the living room. I went over all the things we did to scare the crap out of them. From that day on, we never did talk about Mr. Finchmoore or the prank anymore. In my mind, I felt like some of the trust we had between one another had somehow been taken away. I was hoping that it wasn't because of the prank; however, in my heart, I felt like it was.

A couple weeks after the whole deal, were getting dressed after gym class one morning, getting ready to go to lunch when Jake started pitching one heck of a bitching session. How anyone that claimed to be his friend, his comrades - he liked to use comrade a lot – could do something like this? How anyone could or would steal his jock strap? That jock strap cost his folks one dollar and six cents at the five and dime store. That one dollar and six cent was not an easy thing to come up with these days. How in the world was he going to get his folks to ever spend that much on another jock, so would the Sneaky Sonya please return it.

He walked upstairs to the basketball court and then back down. He was sure that, by then, we would sneak it back and the jock would be on the bench by his locker.

Up the stairs he went, pulling his red and white t-shirt on over his head. We boys looked at him in disbelief as he climbed the stairs. His white, one dollar and six cent jock strap was right there under his shorts, the back strap visible as his shirt fell over it.

Coming back down the stairs, he walked to the bench next to his locker. Nothing being on the bench he turned to look into my eyes and then the eyes of the others. He said, "Well, as much as we have been through together, growing up together, me thinking we were comrades," he really liked that word, "I guess I have been wrong all these years. All it took was a dollar and six cent jock strap for my eyes to be open, open to the world, open to see there is not trust where I have always thought there was trust. Yes, trust and love. Yes, love. I said it, love." He plopped down on the bench and put his head down into his hands.

Bruce walked up behind him, pulled up his t-shirt with his left hand, took hold of the jock strap from the back, and gave it one heck of a pull. He pulled on it hard enough that it raised Jake up off the bench. I'm not real sure if it did his privates any good either.

With that, Bruce yelled at him in a loud voice, "You douche bag."

Chapter 19

Later on that day, after Jake calmed down after all his drama, he came running up to us in somewhat of a panic. A panic to Jake and a panic to someone else, though, was an entirely different deal as the jock strap incident showed quite easily.

"What's up?" I asked Jake and proceeded to wait for him to try to get his breath.

"Well, I was talking to Van Orin a couple of minutes ago, and he has a heck of a deal for us guys," he said to me after his breath evened out to a normal level.

Van Orin was the last name of the kid whose dad ran the funeral home in town. His full name was Tommy Van Orin and he was, what we guys like to call, a real nut. I am not sure, but I believe he was really crazy. Now I'm not talking about crazy like when someone said, this guy or this girl was crazy, meaning they did crazy stuff. No, he was crazy as crazy could get.

The word around town was that he had just gone nuts from being around dead people all his life.

I was told that when his married sister came with her family to visit, they made Tommy sleep in the back room. If there happened to be a dead body in there, all they did was close the coffin and make him a nice, cozy bed on the floor for the night.

I don't know about Tommy, but I can sure enough tell you that if that happened to me, I probably be right on the same level of crazy as him.

Once we had a group of nuns come to town. I still have yet to figure out why nuns, of all people, would be in Verden, Oklahoma. We didn't have a Catholic church in town. For that matter, I'm not even sure if there were any Catholic people in town; however, I guess I wouldn't have known a Catholic if I saw one.

The way the story went: Tommy Van Orin was sitting on the front steps of the funeral home, the place he seemed to always sit. The only time his father made him move from that spot was when someone was coming to see a family member or friend that had died. Other than that, he was always there from daylight until dusk.

It was said that when those nuns walked past the funeral home, Tommy didn't say a word to them. Instead, he jumped up, ran up behind them, grabbed the habit of the nun in the middle, and pulled it up to her waist. Before she knew what had happened, he dropped it and ran back to the protection of the porch. They reported this to his father who, in return, gave him a heck of a beating.

When he was asked why he did it, he said he wanted to know if nuns ever shaved their legs.

Hell, one time was even worse than that. We had show and tell every Friday in school. Each one of us students would have to get up in front of the class to show something and give a little speech about it. Some would bring things like a pet or a ribbon one of their fathers' received in the war. The girls normally brought a lot of things they had sewn up like dressed or bows. Things like that.

One time when it was Tommy's turn, he brought up a wooden bowl covered with a white cloth that had a bright red stripe over it. I was sure he either had a turtle or some kind of a critter in it to talk about.

When he uncovered it, it was a human hand he had gotten from a motorist that had gotten killed on the main highway a couple days back. He had handed the bowl to Sharon Zawacki who always sat in the front row. As she took hold of the bowl, he pulled the cloth off. Looking into the bowl, she froze at first in her seat. Then, all of a sudden, she let out a scream that startled and frightened our teacher, Mrs. Dickens, so much that she leaned back in her chair really fast and fell over.

We didn't see Tommy for a couple weeks after that. Most of us figured that he was either spanked so bad he couldn't come to school, or that his Dad had shipped him off to the loony bin where he needed to be in the first place.

However, a couple of weeks later, he showed up in class just as pretty as you please just as nothing in the world had ever happened. No one ever did find out what happened to that hand. I guess it got taken back and placed with the dead guy.

Either way, anything having to do with Tommy was something that piqued my interest. "Okay Jake, slow down. Tell me. What did Tommy say to you?"

"He told me that his dad has a real live zombie in the funeral parlor," he said, talking as if he had to get the word *zombie* out before it clogged up his throat.

"Bullcrap, there ain't no such in thing as a zombie," I answered him with a 'you're-an-idiot' smile.

"Well I don't know if there is or isn't. Fact is, I don't know all that much about zombies. I'm just going by what Tommy said to me," he answered.

"Well if'n there was such a thing as a zombie, how could you have a real live zombie. I'm not real sure, but in order to be a zombie, one of the major things is being dead. At least, that's what it says in all the books I ever read that had anything at all about zombies in it."

The real truth was, I wasn't sure what it took to be a zombie. I had only read one comic book about such things.

"Tommy told me that his dad picked up this black guy that was from some other country or from down in the swamps of Florida, somewhere there is known to be zombies. I guess he has the guy all sprawled out on some table in one of the back rooms of his funeral home," Jake told us. "He also said that if we could come over around five, when his dad leaves to get some flowers for some funeral, he will take us in to see it… him… the zombie."

It's times like this that a twelve-year-old boy has to do some serious thinking before he answers. I couldn't just jump into a "yes." Lots of things can go wrong with a "yes" spoken too quickly.

First and foremost, anytime you used a "yes" and a "zombie" in the same breath, nothing good could ever come of that.

My being twelve still left a lot of learning on things such as girls and why this or that worked the way it did. Truth be told, my teachers were always telling me, "Boy, you have a long ways to go in school before you will ever amount to much."

At twelve, I sure had me a long ways to go on dead thing especially. Sure, I had seen a lot of dead cows, chickens, birds, and stuff like that. In regards to dead people, though, I sure as hell had whole textbooks to learn. Of course, I did see that dead hand once.

So, before I said sure let's go see the zombie, I wanted to think this thing through completely.

I was almost one hundred percent sure that there was no such a thing as a real zombie. If there were real zombies, then that would, more than likely, make Superman and the likes of super heroes real. In that line of thinking, I can confess that I have never seen Superman come streaking by or jump over big buildings. For that matter, no one I had known had ever seen any super powers in real life, so the chances were fairly good that there was no such thing as zombies.

However, there was always that little part of a person's mind that lies close to the bottom of the brain, the part that tells you, "Who knows? This could be true."

My old grandmother always told me that dead was just that, dead. She said that when a person died, they just naturally went to one of two places: Heaven or Hell. All that was left was the old, used-up body that didn't serve up any more purpose.

Now, I had always put a lot of store in what my grandmother had to say, but I was also under the understanding that anyone could be wrong from time to time. I just didn't want to pay any consequences if this happened to be one of the times she was wrong. With my luck, my grandmother's prediction would be wrong. I would wake up around one or two in the middle of the night, and the dead guy would be sitting on the end of my bed, looking at me. Nope. I would be having none of that—nope, none of that at all.

Chapter 20

With all my thinking and quite a bit of group deliberation, curiosity beat out precaution. There was no way we could say no to seeing something as amazing as a zombie. This was a once in a lifetime experience. Fear was nothing compared to the curiosity and faked bravery of us five boys.

It was all finally decided with one final declaration from Bruce, "Let's do it. Let's go see this zombie." The other guys nodded their heads, but not with all the usual enthusiasm that they had when we were going to play baseball or going to the river to fish.

There was just enough fear in them to make them and me a little paranoid. Not quite enough fear, however, to stop them from wanting to see if this was real.

We all decided to meet with Tommy that evening to see this so called zombie, so we sent Jake with our answer.

We met at the back door of the funeral home straight up at five. Sure enough, Tommy cracked the door open and motioned for us to come in. We had to walk down a short hall. Then we took a left into a room that sure could have used a little more light than the light given off by the candles burning in the room.

There, before us, was a brown and silver coffin. Tommy motioned for us to sit down in the row of chairs that the funeral home always provided for family members and friends.

After we were all sitting down, he said in a whisper, "Okay. I'm going to open the coffin. You all have to be real quit, 'cause I don't want to wake him or anything like that. You never know about zombies."

He could have said anything to us other than, "You never know about zombies." That was like saying, "I hope all goes good, and that he doesn't jump out of his coffin to kill the likes of everyone in the room." At least, that's what, 'You never know about zombies," meant to me.

I finally knew what the guys felt at Mr. Finchmoore's the day we scared the crap out of them, cause if someone was to bump into me or touch me right about then, I would have done one of two things. The first thing was that I would pass plum out. The other was that I would have a major bowl movement right then and there in my jeans.

As Tommy walked over to the coffin, I could think of several hundred places that I would rather be other than where I was at. In truth, I would rather be eating liver with a girl as ugly as all get out. I couldn't even stand the smell of liver cooking.

As Tommy opened the casket front, we saw a large black man lying inside. My mind started repeating, *He is not there. He is not there. That is just an old, worn-out body. He is not there.*

As much as I kept telling myself though, he *was* there, a middle aged black man who I thought at first was fat. When my eyes got more accustomed to the light though, I could see he wasn't fat at all. He seemed to be swollen like when you crack your finger with a hammer or something. That was how he was swollen up, except this wasn't his finger; it was his whole body.

It didn't take me all that long to get my looking done. I was ready to get out of there in a couple seconds.

No one in this world ever told me that there was sometimes air left in the body of someone that had just passed on. Nor did they tell me that if a person has not been embalmed, that their muscles might contract, making an arm or more move on them. Just as I was standing up to leave, touching Jake on the shoulder to indicate that I was ready to get out of there. The black man in the coffin expelled a gosh awful sound out of his body along with sitting up part of the way, jerking a couple of times before relaxing back into the coffin. Now, I don't know for sure what happened to the other guys, because in my panic to get away from sure zombie death, I ran into a large brass pot standing by the door, knocking me out. My next realization of life was in the kitchen with a cool rag over a knot on my forehead about the size of a right large chicken egg.

I came to as Mr. Van Orin asked me if I felt better or if I needed him to call my folks to come get me.

I couldn't answer for a couple seconds. As I came to my senses, I knew better than to let him call anyone in my family. I would have knots on my bottom as large, if not larger, than the one now on my head.

"My friends?" I asked as the link from my brain to my mouth finally reengaged.

"You were all alone when I found you," he answered.

I knew then that I had been left lying on the floor, bleeding like a stuck hog, knocked out, or dead for all that matter. They left me to be killed or eaten. Whatever a zombie does to people, I'm not all too sure.

Well, the truth was that if I had not hit my head, I would have done the same thing probably.

Come to find out after talking to Mr. Van Orin, the dead guy was not a zombie. He was just a guy that fell into the river and drowned himself, because his folks never taught him anything about swimming.

I don't think anyone saw Tommy again that summer. Next time we saw him was a couple days after school started. He walked into math class, carrying a paper sack. The teacher took that away from him and inspected it before he could even find a seat. I guess she didn't want another hand showing up around her classroom. Come to find out, it was just his ham sandwich, a small bag of chips, and an apple he had been eating on the way to school.

We more or less left him alone after that, but he always smiled from ear to ear when he saw one of us, especially me.

Chapter 21

One night when we boys were scheming up a way to get back at Tommy, my grandmother came out and asked, "Any of you boys seen Mr. Ditmer's duck, Lonnie?"

We all looked up at her, shaking our heads no.

"Well, that darn duck is missing. It sure wouldn't hurt you no-accounts one little bit to get off your back sides to go see if'n you can help him find that fool duck," she said, not talking to one of us "no-accounts" or another.

Mr. Ditmer was an old man who lived out North of town in, what we like to call, the mountains. In reality, the place was no more than three large hills, each facing the road with a cliff from five to the larger twenty feet. We boys had killed many foreign enemies in the battles we had had there.

Mr. Ditmer lived a few hundred yards from the smallest hill. He had a pet duck that he called Lonnie. It wasn't much of a duck to look at. Every time we boys walked by Mr. Ditmer's house, Lonnie would attack us, trying to peck one of us on the leg. At least, he would try flying the best he could at us, trying to scare us.

We were sure Mr. Ditmer must have always seen us boys walking up the road, because Lonnie always seemed to be out of the coop when we walked by. It had to be just some small form of entertainment for Mr. Ditmer, watching that duck flap over to us, squawking. At very least, he must have heard that damn duck and poked his head out to see what the ruckus was.

In truth, Mr. Ditmer really didn't care all that much for Lonnie. What he *did* care for was how Lonnie could attract other ducks, any kind of duck, from wild geese flying over to about anything that resembled a duck. As long as the bird had feathers on it, they seemed to like it around Lonnie.

What Mr. Ditmer did was keep Lonnie away from any water at all, other than drinking water. He kept him locked up in the chicken coop with all his chickens, something Lonnie seemed to not care about one way or the other. However, when Mr. Ditmer got a craving for duck, he would load Lonnie in his old black Ford truck and head for the small lake south of town.

Lonnie was more like an old bird dog than a duck. When he saw that black truck back up to the coop, he went to running back and forth in that pin, bobbing his head up and down. If there was anything Lonnie liked in this world, it was swimming. On the way to the lake, you could hear Lonnie for miles, quacking and quacking, knowing he would soon be swimming.

Then, when they got there, Lonnie would get in the water and swim for hours on end. All the while, Mr. Ditmer sat in the bushes with his shotgun, waiting on some un-expecting duck to land nearby. Usually it didn't take long at all before a duck would come along to quench Mr. Ditmer's craving for a duck supper.

As we walked up to Mr. Ditmer's house to help fetch that darned bird, here came Lonnie, just like all the other times, to peck and fly at us. Only difference was that, this time, Mr. Ditmer was right behind him.

"Boys, this is awful nice of you young'uns to come help look for Lonnie. The darnful duck was in the Packard I have out back," he said to us boys.

Seems Mr. Ditmers had a Packard car out back of his house. It was all rusty; no one even knew if the thing ran or not. At least, no one had ever seen him driving it.

"I reckon there was a hole in the wire around the chicken house. Lonnie either found the hole or watched some of them old laying hens get through. He's been just sitting in that old car," he said.

"Get back, Lonnie. Leave these boys alone. They done come to help find ya. They are friends," he gave the duck a little kick to shut him up. "Come on up to the porch, boys, and I'll get us some lemonade."

We all sat down around his porch, trying to find some shade. I sat on an old, rusty milk can. Charlie sat on the steps. Gary sat on the side of the porch. Bruce tried to sit on the can next to me until I pushed him away while he slapped at me. He changed his mind after that and sat next to Gary. Jake made a nice place on the grass at the foot of the steps.

When Mr. Ditmer brought the drinks out, the results weren't too great. I didn't want to be rude, but it was terrible. There was no sign of sugar anywhere near my glass or had there ever been. The only thing that gave you a reason to call it lemonade was that it had a whole lemon in it. It wasn't a whole cut up lemon, but a complete whole lemon with no sign of a cut anywhere on it. What we boys had were glasses of water with a lemon in each.

Sitting down amongst us boys, Mr. Ditmer said, "Boys, once again I sure want to thank you for coming all the way up here to help find Lonnie. I just don't know what I would ever do without him. I know he ain't much good for nothing 'cept swimming around, but I sure need me that duck."

We didn't tell him that someone had told us that the only reason he wanted Lonnie around was to be his living decoy.

"I was sure as the world that some of them older kids had done strung Lonnie up," he said as he tried to slap a fly that had just landed on his cheek.

"Strung up? You mean like hanged?" Gary asked.

"Sure, he meant like hanged, hanged like they did them cattle rustlers and murderers." Bruce answered.

"Sure, strung up means hanged; but, when I said strung up, I meant with chicken fat or fat from a cow," he answered, smiling to us while still swatting at the persistent fly.

"Chicken fat? What ya mean chicken fat?" I asked, looking around in question to the other boys. I noticed that they didn't care for their so called Lemonade either.

"You mean to tell me that you four boys sitting right here on my porch never strung no ducks up?" he asked, slapping his leg. I wasn't sure if it was at the fly or just because he got a kick out of us not hearing of what he was talking about. "What in the world has this old world come to when four boys, near grown, got no clue whatsoever about stringing ducks? Darn near unbelievable!"

I really had no clue what he was talking about, but the part where he said we were near grown sure made me perk up.

"Well, you boys gather around a bit, because I am fixing to let you in on something that has been known since them pharaohs back in the olden days. Heck, who's to know, stringing ducks might even have been done back in the day people were living in caves, back when they were wondering when they would be able to invent something to make their steaks and pork chops taste a bit better?

"I guess eating steak and pork chops straight off the cow would be a little bit bland. That's not to mention all the diseases it could cause in the body, not being cooked and all. Them old cave guys sure enough ate it that way, though. I'm sure.

"The problem with them cave people was they had no fire or electric stuff, so they had themselves no clue about cooking food. I have spent many a night wondering how in the world they ever ate pinto beans or potatoes and such having no fire to do some cooking with. You boys every seen pinto beans 'fore they was cooked? Well, them babies is hard as a rock," he said, picking up his half empty glass of so-called lemonade.

"I'm not even real sure when they invented fire for cooking. For all I know, it could be back when them Romans was running hitter and skitter around the country, trying to conquer ever one they laid eyes on. That, or they was beating up on Christians and anybody else they could talk into getting into that big football looking dome they built.

I was almost sure he wasn't about to get into his story at all. I was about ready to stand up and tell him we had to be getting home when he finally got into it.

"When I was not much older than you boys, I had the record around these parts for stringing ducks. I had me twenty-two of the critters strung up," he said, placing the glass at his feet.

"Stringing ducks is easy enough. All you got to do is get you a piece of fat off a steak or some chicken fat you might find lying around when your folks fry a chicken. Steak fat is easier, though. After someone eats a T-bone or whatever, there is always the fat they cut off the meat.

"After you get your fat, you go down to a pond or lake, anywhere there is a duck. It makes not a bit of difference what kind of duck they are as long as they are a bit tame, tame enough for them to come up to you to beg for bread crumbs or something or other. You take that piece of fat, tie it on a piece of fishing twine and throw it to one of them un-expecting ducks. As soon as he scarfs it up, it will pass right through him, faster than you can say hot dog," he said, a bit cheesy smile spread over his face.

"You boys ever heard someone say, 'Wow that was faster than grease through a duck?'" he asked, looking to Jake first, then each one of us. Seeing no reaction on our faces, he went back to his story.

"Just as soon as that fat passes through that duck and ends back up on the ground, another duck will see it lying there and scarf it up as well. That all leaves the first duck with the fishing line in its mouth and coming out its behind. When the other duck eats it, well it does the same thing. This goes on and on until you got yourself several ducks all strung out on that fishing line. It doesn't seem to hurt them none. Once you cut the fat off the last duck, you can pull the line out, no problem. They'll swim off on their merry way. Like I said, 'fore I had me twenty-two ducks all strung up and tied to a tree. I never did find out who cut them loose; but, next morning, I took Tommy down to show him, and they was all gone," he said, standing up.

First I looked at Jake, then Charlie, then the others. If a person had seen our faces, right then you would have known that stringing ducks was in our not-too-distance future.

On the way home, Bruce said, "We are having stake tonight. I'll save the fat. You guys game?"

That was like asking us if we wanted to breathe. Of course we were game.

We decided to meet at the little pond in the park around eight the next morning with the steak fat to see if old man Ditmer was telling the truth or not. If it was true, maybe we could break his record. If not, at least it was something we could do or - should I say - had to try.

The next morning, we all met at the pond. Bruce had some steak fat in a mason jar. Jake had brought some green fishing line that he had taken off his dad's fishing pole. We tied the fat on the line as tight as we could so it wouldn't come off before it got completely through the duck.

We all started jumping around, waving our arms above our heads, calling out, "Duck! Here, duck! Come on, you old ducks, you! We are over here, ready to feed you ducks."

There weren't but about eight ducks in the pond, but sure enough, they started swimming toward us. They were coming quite quickly to eat whatever we had. We hadn't been smart enough to bring bread to entice them any, but stealing bread wasn't all that easy. Food wasn't that easy to come by, so our folks watched it closely.

Jake picked up some grass and tossed it into the water. The ducks, thinking it was food, went back in the water after it.

"Now! Now!" I shouted to Bruce, "Throw it now!"

Bruce tossed the fat right in front of a big white duck that went after it as if it was duck gold. He got it in his beak, threw his head back, and swallowed. Sure enough, it went down his throat in one big piece, no problem. We boys must have looked nuts, us trying to get behind that duck to see what of that fat came out.

It had to be less than a minute and there it was, floating on the water. When another duck saw it, he did the same as the first. In less than ten minutes, we had eight ducks all strung up on the same line.

We boys were so excited about what we had done that we were jumping, slapping each other on the backs, and yelling things. I'm not even sure what we said in the excitement.

We never did break Mr. Ditmer's record, but, for the rest of the summer, if any of us had chicken or steak for supper, you can bet we were at the pond the next day. We did it so often that when the ducks saw us coming to the pond, they just started getting into a line.

Chapter 22

We had a kid in town named Johnny Bric who was a couple years older than us boys. I wasn't sure of his age, but I bet he was around fourteen or fifteen. I couldn't tell by the grade he was in, because I was told he had been held back several times because of his grades and cussing. About anything that would hold a kid back held Johnny back.

People said he was held back in the sixth grade, not because of his grades, because, for the first time in his life, he was carrying the average grade of D. He was held back, because he skipped a total of thirty-six days that year. So, he just barely had a passing grade, but not enough days on the books to pass on.

Johnny was your typical bully, picking on guys that were smaller than he was. People said bullies were either from a bad family, had an inferiority complex, whatever that was, or were just misunderstood. I think they left out what I call, "the big one," though. Some of the bullies are just plain mean. At least, in Johnny's case, he was just pure mean.

He would walk up behind someone carrying one or a bunch of books and grab them from behind, making the person lose their grip and let go of anything they were holding. He would also wait for a person to walk by so he could throw dirt, dog poop, cat poop, and, if he could get a hold of it, people poop on them.

Even more, he gave the teachers nothing but grief. I believe the only reason any teacher passed him on was just to get him out of their classroom.

Sure, we boys played a lot of pranks, but I can't remember anytime we did anything to hurt anyone. Not Johnny. If he could make a person bleed, make a person cry, or cost them any kind of money, then he loved it. He just loved being mean.

That summer, Johnny was in rare form. He gave Gary a bloody nose because Gary was wearing a red shirt. He said red made him mad, made him go crazy. He said it would be to our advantage if none of us wore red anymore. You can bet none of us did.

He beat me up that summer as well, because I was laughing at something Jake said to me. It wasn't even about him. We didn't see him standing in the alley by the bank. That afternoon, by the depot, he caught up with me and whipped me like there was not going to be a tomorrow.

When I went home and my Grandmother saw what shape I was in, she picked up my Louisville Slugger. She said that she was on her way to beat the heck out of Johnny, Johnny's father, and any other relative that might be there at the time.

It took a lot of pulling on her dress, pleading, and crying to stop her, because she was like a grandmother possessed. Finally, though, she settled down and saw it my way.

A boy in a fight had to take his lumps and go on. He sure couldn't let one of his parents take up his fight. For God's sake, his Grandmother fighting would have been the worst for my reputation. I would never ever live the words down: sissy, pussy, and mommy's boy.

I would have taken another beating before I would ever let anyone call me a sissy, pussy, or mommy's boy. Nope, sure didn't want any of that.

Like my mother would always say, "Boy, watch what you do, 'cause what goes around sure enough comes back around." Over all the times I've paid for my stupid actions, I have come to believe just that.

Now, just a few days, maybe a week before school started, a family moved in across the street from the grain elevator. The only thing that set them apart from others in town was the way they dressed. They all wore different shades of light-blue in their respective styles. The mother wore a plain dress all the way down to her ankles with a small black hat or black cap on her head. Her daughter's dress was also all the way down. She didn't wear a cap on her head like her mother, though. The little brother wore plain dark blue pants and a light blue long sleeve shirt just as his father did.

I asked my grandmother about them. She said they sounded like Mennonites to her, but she would have to see them to be sure. I had me no idea what a Mennonite was. They could be some kind of an Indian tribe or anything for that matter.

Jake's father told us one afternoon that they were a religious bunch. He said that Mennonites, more than not, stayed among themselves. He apparently had never seen a Mennonite family living in no town, because, to be a Mennonite, it was a rule that a person had to live pretty barebones which normally meant that they would stay with people of their own type.

Mennonites had to take their radios out of their cars. They could never have white-wall tires on their cars either, and they had to own a least one cow. That cow had to be a milk-giving cow as well, because the Mennonite women were taught to cook from a day or two after they were born into this world.

He went on to tell us that he come across a Mennonite family once when he was quail hunting. They kicked him off their land, but, before they did, they gave him a loaf of bread and two cinnamon rolls. He added that those had to be the best cinnamon rolls he had ever put his lips around. They were so good that they didn't even make it down to his stomach. They just dissolved on the way down. For the bread, he had to set a can of pork in beans on it to keep it from floating off someplace since it was so soft and fluffy.

I only believed about half of what his father said, though. Jake's father was known to stretch the truth somewhat. All he had told us about the Mennonites I took with a grain of salt. We boys, being the boys we were, made a point in meeting the Mennonite family. Walking past their home one afternoon, we saw the boy was picking weeds out of the little flower bed by the porch. His Sister was sitting on the steps with a glass of what looked like water.

I walked up to them and said, "Hi," having been elected as the one who would talk first. The girl gave us a nice little smile and said 'hi' back. Her little brother turned his head to look up at us. He didn't smile. He just nodded his head slightly in what I took, or hoped, meant 'hi.' The looks on the girl's face told us that she was not real happy we were there. Her little brother just went back to weeding, though, paying us no mind.

"My name is Sonny. These boys are Jake, Charlie, Gary, and Bruce," I said to her, pointing to each guy one at a time.

"My name is Sara Ann Mathews. That is my brother, Mathew," she answered, giving us all a once over in turn.

"What's your brother's first name," I asked her.

"Mathew," she said, looking at me strangely.

"I thought your last name was Mathews," I replied, raising my ball cap with one hand, scratching my head with the other.

"It is. His first name is also Mathew. His full name is Mathew Erin Mathews. We just call him Mathew. Still confused?"

I wasn't so much confused. I could see why she would ask, though, as the others all looked a little dumbfounded. My face was probably the same. I was just surprised because I had never met anyone with the same first and last name.

Well, maybe this was a Mennonite thing that they did with the boys. Heck, I sure didn't know. These were the first Mennonites I had ever talked to. Truth be told, these were the first Mennonites I had ever laid eyes on.

Sara Ann seemed like she was warming up to us boys somewhat, not looking as annoyed as she first seemed. We found out that they had bought a farm several miles out of town. They were only staying here for a month or so, giving the people they bought the farm from time to move out. The farm they bought was a dairy farm. I didn't say anything, but I thought maybe Jake's dad knew more than people gave him credit for.

After finding out this piece of information, Sara's mother came out on the porch to see what was going on. She was a real friendly woman, offering us a glass of lemonade and some fudge. I know for a fact that none of us guys ever passed up a piece of fudge. That would be like a sin or something.

Again Jakes Dad was right. That had to be about the best fudge I had ever tasted in my entire life. Eating that fudge, talking to Sara, and seeing her smile, I was about ready to go cut the radio antenna off of my mother's car, save my money, and buy a milk cow too. I'd straight up move in with this family.

We laughed and joked for at least an hour or more. I made it up in my mind that, if I ever got a chance, I was going to go to a Mennonite church someday to see if all the Mennonites were as nice as these folks.

Then it happened. Charlie said, "Oh, crap."

As I looked around, I saw that Johnny was coming down the sidewalk. I knew it was too late to walk away or even run. I could see excitement in Johnny's eyes. The excitement was because he knew he was getting ready to have a nice session of messing with all us boys.

"What ya girls doing?" he asked while walking up the last few steps up to us.

"We're just talking about stuff," Gary said to him, not looking him in the eyes.

"Why are you talking to these Jews, Amish, or whatever the heck they are?" he asked.

"They're not Jews or Amish. They are Mennonites," I said while hoping I wouldn't be the one catching his wrath.

"Jews, Amish, Mennonites, it makes no difference. They are still people who good people shouldn't be around," he said, glaring over to Sara.

I wanted to say, "Get out of here, you big lummox," but I didn't. I was man enough to admit to myself that I was afraid I would get another beating. That being said, a beating was sure bad enough, but a beating in front of a girl? I would never be able to face her or my friends again.

In the end, I didn't say anything. Well, I didn't say anything that he could hear, but I was screaming plenty to him in my mind.

"What are you Mennonites doing in town? I thought you people lived out on farms and such - stuck to yourselves."

"We are waiting to move to our farm," she answered; her smile showed me that she had heard nothing about this evil boy.

"Well my old man tells me you Mennonite folks don't fight. Hell, he said you all don't do nothing for anyone other than your own kind," he said, smiling as if he had just delivered the Gettysburg address.

"In the war, you all just went up in them hills or stayed on the farm and let all the others do your fighting for you," he said, trying to provoke some anger out of her.

"I have no idea what went on in the war," she answered. Her face twisted and her voice mixed to show her own disgust.

"Well, I don't like Mennonites one little bit. In fact, next time I see you, I may just beat you and your brother up like you was plain people." He smiled and laughed to himself just loud enough so that we could hear it. He was always about getting a response out of anyone and everyone.

Without as much as a by-your-leave, he hauled off and kicked Sara's little brother. It wasn't hard enough to hurt him, but it was hard enough, however, to make him let out a little yelp.

That was all it took for me. I jumped up, ready to get me another beating. I had to do something, even if it caused me some pain. I had to at least act like a man, even if I was scared enough to pee my pants.

I heard it before I knew what happen. *Crack.* I could always tell when someone was hit. I've never heard a tooth break, but there's always a sound that lets me know that something's going down.

The sound was a whole lot more than that scary sound.

One second, Tommy was standing there talking about how tough he was. The next thing I saw was Tommy on the ground, blood running from his nose. He had a look of utter surprise on his face as he stumbled backward, gripping his own nose and falling backwards to safety. His look was only the look a person sees when he sneaks up behind another person and grabs a handful of their leg, hollering, "Got you." When they finally turn around, that's the same look that Tommy had.

He lay on the ground, tears starting to well up in his eyes. Sara walked slowly over him, both fists still doubled up.

"Let me tell you something you big dumb Bully, you. I don't know if Mennonites fought in the war. Fact is, I don't know all that much about Mennonites either. I pray I will know more as life goes on because I am trying to be a good Mennonite," she said, her voice holding more anger than any girl I had ever heard.

We boys looked to one another. I'd heard about the cat getting your tongue. Well, that old cat could have had a field day with tongues as all of ours were hanging out - hanging way out.

"When I say trying to be a good Mennonite that is just what I mean: *trying.* You see, I haven't been one all that long. Before my parents decided to become Mennonites, we were just like you are what you call normal people. That's all except for one little detail. My father was a member of the United States Marines. He fought all across the pacific. He's got more battle ribbons than you got teeth, you big dummy, you." she said still standing over him.

Tommy was just holding his nose, trying to stop the bleeding and trying to hold back his tears as well. He wasn't having success doing either.

"And another thing. When my dad got back from the war, he taught new Marine recruits how to defend themselves. I guess some of that training must have rubbed off on me." She stepped away from him.

With that, Tommy jumped to his feet and took off running and screaming "I'm going to tell my mommy on you."

From that day on, we never had another lick of trouble from tommy-boy. All it took to take the bully out of the bully was a head strong Mennonite girl that was raised by a Marine. I think she was waiting on some person to finally prove herself. Change is never a thing that is easy to come by or adjust to.

Chapter 23

Our American History teacher, Mrs. Smythe had a fourteen year old daughter, Daisy, who could hold her own with any of the boys when it came to things I liked to call, "Boy things," running, softball, baseball, and she could even fight if the need be. She was an all-around good guy, I believed. A guy until I really saw her. When I first really saw her standing by the bleachers during a high school football game, I went from young, no-account, lazy kid (as my Grandmother liked to call me from time to time), to a young, no-account, lazy kid in love.

When she pulled her red baseball cap off and shook her long, black hair out, I would have done about anything just to stand close and look.

When Charlie saw me looking at her with my mouth wide open in a half comatose daze, he said, "What the hell are you looking at?" With a gawk, he answered himself, "You're looking at Mrs. Smythe's daughter. You've gone plum buggers over a girl."

Turning to the other boys, he screamed a little too loud, just loud enough for Daisy to hear, "Guys come here. Sonny has gone plum nuts over a girl," he said pointing at Daisy.

She turned her head, looking first at Charlie, him having just screamed loud enough that half the people in the stands turned their heads to see what was going on.

"Shut up, shit head," I hissed at him, grabbing the sleeve of his shirt. He took it as the opposite. "Yep, Sonny is sure enough in love with Daisy standing right over there by the bleachers."

Bruce chimed as well, "Are you talking about our American History teacher's daughter, Daisy? Daisy with a D?"

"Yep, that's the one. Sure as hell is, that girl right there," Charlie said, still pointing at Daisy.

Me pulling Charlie away, we started walking toward town. "Good Gosh almighty man. Why would you say something like that? I was only staring, trying to make out if she was a boy or a girl. That's all," I said hoping the fellows would buy that answer.

Gary laughed in reply, "If you were having a problem trying to decide if Daisy was a girl or was sure enough a boy, then bubba you can bet your sweet butt that I'll not be spending the night with you anymore. You sure enough have to be queer as a three dollar bill if you can't. I can't trust my virtue to you at all, not at all, at all."

I believe that was the first time in my life I wanted to forever be rid of these guys. I knew I would never be able to show my face around Daisy again. First, because I thought she was so darn good looking, downright pretty. Second, because I didn't know how she would take what just happened. There might be a heck of a good chance that the next time I saw her, she would beat the crap out of me in front of God and all my friends, something I could never live with.

The next time I did see her, I was walking to the store to get Granny some Garrett snuff. As I opened the door to the shop, she stepped out. There we stood looking eye to eye for what seemed like an hour. I didn't know if she was fixing to cock me beside the head with the Morton Salt she had in her right hand, but I knew that whatever happened, I was pretty much a goner. Either it would be the Morton or one heck of a tongue lashing.

She just stood, looking at me for a couple of seconds, and then turned and started walking away. When she was a few feet away, she turned and said a single word, "Girl."

Chapter 24

We had a hay ride to day camp and back right around Halloween time. That was the next time I had anything to do with Daisy. To tell the truth, I had avoided her as much as possible in school or around town. I still wasn't sure if she was over the remarks had I made. I don't consider myself a coward. I did, however, live by the rule, "Out of sight, out of mind." In those days, I figured if I had no contact with her, there wasn't much chance she could embarrass me in front of any of my friends.

I had it in the back of my mind at the time that she was just lying in wait She was like one of the tigers you read about in National Geographic, ready to spring on you with no mercy at all. Instead of using fangs and claws like a tiger, she would use words that could cut me as deep as the fangs from a tiger.

When I saw her at the water fountain or coat rack, just walking down the hall, I always went the other way or hid in one of the doorways until she passed. It made me late for class several times, but at least I still had my pride.

Now, day camp was where several of the different classes got together with a couple of the teachers, and went to a small park in town. You could hardly call it a park, actually. There was a slide that had no ladder to the top, the steps having long since rusted away. The merry go round wouldn't turn; and there was an old swing set made from old tires that only had one working. The centerpiece was a large green turtle with a big rusty spring holding it up that would make it sway back and forth. Its head was long gone. We figured it must have rusted off long ago; or someone took a disliking to the turtle and beat its head off with a large blunt object.

We boys only showed up for the hay ride for the hot dogs and hamburgers. We had our usual rubber snakes, plastic spiders, and pretty much everything we would need to put the fear of God into all the young ladies that were unlucky enough to come along.

There were several boys and girls already on the wagon, waiting to go. I stood around, waiting for the others to all climb on, wanting to wait until the last moment to get on. It's because I knew the horse that pulled the wagon was old sway back, Randy.

Randy had to be the meanest critter of a horse ever put on this earth. If you walked by her, she would stare at you with those big, sad looking brown eyes, making you want to pet her forehead. As soon as you started rubbing on that head, though, she would bite the living crap out of you, then start whinnying. It was a whinny like a laugh. I believe she stood in her stall waiting, hoping someone would walk by that didn't know her.

Hell, last year, old Randy took off running. It must have been a heck of a sight, kids hanging on for dear life, screaming at top of their lungs. None of the kids were hurt, but it had to be a sorry picnic with wet underpants.

That is why I wanted to be one of the last on. If old Randy pulled anything, I wanted to be at the back of the wagon, a good place to get off in a hurry.

When it looked like he was about ready to pull away, I climbed on. There wasn't much room by then with all the kids that were going this year. Sitting in the one and only spot left, I felt a little security that near the back until I started looking around.

On my left was nose picker, Mike Hussey, a guy that picked his nose always; and I mean always. Teacher called him up front to read something out of our American History book; and the whole time he read, he was holding the book with his left hand, and picking his nose with his right.

Sitting behind me was Opal Eiller. She never talked much, which we all found strange. Her dad owned the only clinic in town; and we boys thought that if our folks ran the only clinic, we would have enough material to talk about until all the cows came home. Not her, she just did her school work .

Beside Opal was Susan Legner. Susan was a talker. It made no difference what people were talking about, Susan could join right in. In fact, she was talking about cooking hotdogs right then, about not ever under-cooking a hot dog. As she put it, under-cooking them could, and would, cause your children some kind of deformity. She wasn't quite sure what the deformity was, but she just knew under-cooked Hot Dogs caused it.

Smiling, I turned to see who she was talking to. To my surprise and dismay, it was Daisy. When I looked over, our eyes met. Even faster than what they say about Superman and that speeding bullet, well I was faster than that as I looked away.

Right then, I wanted to jump off the back of that old wagon. Heck, I wished and hoped in that short second that Randy would just run like there wasn't going to be no tomorrow. Throw me the heck off that stupid wagon. Throw me away from Nose Picker, Opal, and Susan Legner. Most of all, throw me away from Daisy

I said a short prayer to myself, "God I know I've done several bad – no, not bad - rotten things in my life. If you can see your way to forgive me, find me just a little spot in Heaven, then I am sure enough ready to go." I shut my eyes. I had never been killed before, didn't know if it hurt or not, but I was ready just in case it did.

No such luck, Randy stayed at a nice slow steady pace. Nothing like death or a broken leg would save me. I had to set right there next to Daisy. So close in fact, that when Daisy talked back to Susan, I could feel her breath on the side of my face.

The rest of the ride to the park, all I could do was watch the dust coming from the back of the wagon wheels, and pray that something terrible would soon happen to either me or that stupid wagon.

When we finally reached the park, she must have thought I was dying to go to the bathroom or something. I jumped off that stupid old wagon fast enough to send me into a tripping run as I set off to the swing set.

I sat in the only half-decent swing, head down, feeling like the coward I was being afraid of a girl. I don't know what I was running from either. Maybe I thought I'd have her yelling at me in front of the whole school. Who knows? Maybe she'd try to whip me in front of my own friends, and part of me thought she might stand a chance.

Looking up, I saw Daisy heading in my direction. I was hoping she was going to stop to talk to one of the other girls on the way, but I knew better. Her eyes were fixed on me and me alone. I thought of maybe running, but running was almost as bad as getting whipped in front of everyone. The only advantage of running is that, if she did take a swing, at least I didn't have to put up with the pain of being hit.

When she got to within three feet of me, I stood up. For some reason, I believed there was less pain if you are standing. I have no idea where that came from, though. I guess the truth of my standing was just in case my fear and shame won out, and I made good on the running.

"What are you doing?" she asked me.

"Nothing" I lied. My Grandmother always told me there was absolutely no reason to ever tell a lie. Apparently, my Grandmother had never been in a situation quite like this. "I'm supposed to meet the other guys here," I said, looking around as if I expected them to be only a few yards away.

"I've been wanting to talk to you," she said, looking me straight in the eyes.

"You have? I wished I had known that. I would have come found you," I lied again like a man trying to keep from sitting his butt down in an electric chair.

"You remember what happened at the ball game?" she asked.

"No," it had come to the end. My heart was beating like someone was about to pull the lever to send me to heaven.

I wanted to fake a heart attack, but I couldn't remember what the signs of a heart attack were. Should I fall down, close my eyes, and just lay there. Should I start shaking first and then fall, or should I scream, "Help," and then grab my chest and fall. That just brought up another problem, in a panic I wasn't sure where the heart was. I knew the general area of the heart, but in a case like this, I could not afford to grab the wrong part of my body.

I guess my grandmother was right when she told me if I didn't pay more attention in class, it would come back to haunt me sometime.

"You know when Charlie and your other friends were teasing you about liking me?"

"Oh, that! They were just fooling around," trying to brush it off as best as I could and still not pass out.

"You mean you don't like me? Don't think I'm pretty?" she asked, shifting her weight to the other leg.

My grandma always talked about being put in between a rock and a hard place. I understood in that second with that rock placed square on top.

After some deliberation, I belted out, "I think you're pretty." If she could read between the lines, that mean, I think about you all the time. I think you're so darn pretty that my mind just stops working and gets all fuzzed up when you're around.

"You like me?" she asked in no uncertain terms.

Do you like me? Now that was a biggie. It could change the whole course of my life. I wasn't sure, but I think I was about to be thrust into manhood. My life would be over as I knew it. Would I ever be able to play baseball again? Could a guy play baseball with a girl on his mind? That seemed like it would be taking an awful big risk when his mind wasn't completely on the game. He could get cold cocked by a baseball, or, even worse, hit with a Louisville slugger upside his head.

"Yes, I like you," I said with the ever so slightest mumble so she I could deny it later if needed.

"Stop your mumbling. Give me a yes or no. Do you like me?"

She must have known that trick, too.

"Yes, yes, I like you. I like you a lot. More than you know." In less time than it takes for a baseball to go from the pitcher's mound to the batter, I had become a man. No more would I ever be able to goof off with my friends. Like it said in the Bible, when a boy becomes a man, he has to look away from boy things and look after man things.

I guess that meant I would start getting hair on my chest and in other places. I wouldn't be able to take a shower with the other guys after gym class, because they would know I had crossed over.

Daisy stood there, looking at me for what seemed like forever with a grin on her face. Then without a word or anything, she reached over, took hold of my hand, and gave me a real quick kiss on the mouth. "I like you a lot, too," she said, and then left.

Chapter 25

We boys were setting around Charlie's house one afternoon when Charlie said, "Well, of all people."

His first cousin, on his dad's side, came driving up, stepped out of the car and said, "Well hello, Charlie boy."

Charlie's cousin was more or less the black sheep of the family. If you could pick one person out of his family to be a black sheep, my grandmother would have picked everyone in Charlie's family. They all fit the bill for a black sheep, counting Charlie's mother amongst them.

Many were the times that she would get mad at someone or something, go into a fit, buy a bottle of moonshine, and get tossed into jail for cussing someone out. She even got sent to the police once for throwing a rock through Mrs. Smilie's window because Mrs. Smilie's gate swung open to the sidewalk side, causing her to bump into it in her drunken stupor.

She picked up a rock and chucked it through Mrs. Smilie's front picture window, screaming at the top of her lungs, "You old bitty. Don't you know any better than to have a gate that swings out into the street where's God and anyone else that happens by can get all wrapped up in it, near killing themselves just like I almost did."

Picking up another rock and chucking it through the broken window, she knocked off the UHF control on Mrs. Smilie's new 13 inch television set.

Mrs. Smilie grabbed up the phone, telling the ladies on the party line to get the heck off the line and get off right then and there. She had a crazy woman on her hands, chucking rocks at her.

I guess Mrs. Smilie got the law okay, because Charlie's mom was sweeping the main street the next afternoon. If you couldn't pay your two dollar public drunken fine, the law made you work it off, cleaning up the park or, in this case, sweeping the streets.

"Brought you a present," Charlie's cousin said, walking past the rest of us.

Charlie wasn't all that fond of his cousin Jan. Jan would come and go like we changed our underpants, four sometime even five times in the same week.

When Charlie would get to liking having Jan around, the man would up and leave, not saying a word to anybody. He'd just up and leave. Half the time, he wouldn't even pack up his things, leaving them right where he took them off. That or he'd just pile his stuff up. It had to be hard on Charlie, Jan promising to do things with him. He'd always promise to go fishing, camping, or all sorts of stuff. After that, he'd just be gone in the next instant.

"What you bring me?" Charlie asked him.

"It's in my trunk," Jan said to him, tossing him the car keys.

We boys walked out to his car and watched Charlie insert the key to open the trunk. To our surprise, there was an old wooden crate marked Mrs. Turner's homemade beets. However, there were no beets in this box. It was plum full of firecrackers. Really, it was plum full.

There were several packages of Black Cat firecrackers, some sparklers, and numerous other things that set all our faces to wide, wide smiles. The sparklers were for girls or little kids in diapers, not guys like us, but the other things were lighting our imaginations up like July the fourth. Several roman candles were mixed in. I kind of liked those the best, because we could hold those while they shot all different color balls into the air or whatever you happen to be pointing them at.

At the bottom of the box, though, there was a brilliant surprise. We had come upon the mother lode of firecrackers. It was chock full of cherry bombs and tin can firecrackers. Tin cans and cherry bombs were the type of firecrackers that would not just blow the tip of your finger off. These babies would blow your whole hand off if you were unlucky enough to be holding onto one when it decided to explode.

We knew Jan must have been coming from somewhere in Texas, because tin cans and cherry bombs had been outlawed in Oklahoma a couple of years before. At least, that is what my grandmother said anyway. My grandmother had a bad habit of blaming things on the state of Oklahoma when she wanted something or didn't want something, and she needed some kind of an excuse.

She told me once that she was going to fix me a pineapple upside-down cake. I loved that kind of cake. When I came home, mouth-watering for a piece of upside-down cake and found nothing where it should be cooling, I asked what had happened. She told me that the state had put a moratorium on upside-down Pineapple cakes, because the people in Hawaii were throwing a fit about something or other.

She told me once more that I couldn't get a new pair of cowboy boots because the state was tired of people coming up from Texas and causing trouble. So, Oklahoma stopped selling anything that made us look like we had come from Texas.

Hell, once she told me that, if any kid under the age of eighteen was caught getting in trouble more than twice, the state passed a law that they had to be shipped to Mexico for the summer to help the Mexicans make tacos to send to the United States.

I walked the straight and narrow for a few days after that because you can bet your last dollar that I had me no desire to end up in some town in Mexico cooking tacos on some stove made out of clay. No matter what she said though, a boy of twelve can come up with more things to do with a plain old stick then you can imagine. So, when all these firecrackers fell into our hands, our thoughts were running wild. We started planning from the first second we saw those things. I could feel the juices in each of our heads. The combined force was probably enough to set off a tank.

Mr. Weedomire had bought a brand new Hudson car just recently. He loved that brown and white Hudson. It was out, sun shining on it, a couple of hours a day, every day. If it looked like rain, he would drive it into the garage and not bring it out until, not just the rain had stopped, but the roads had all dried off.

Bruce thought it would be funny if, when he started the car to make his daily run to the post office, we threw a black cat under the car to make it sound like the motor itself was blowing up.

We hid in the weeds the very next day. When Mr. Weedomire got in the car, as he did every morning at nine am to go get his mail, we tossed a firecracker under his car. Pop, it went, just as he turned the key. Shutting the car off, he got out to raise the hood. He scratched the back of his head as he looked at the motor.

Seeing nothing out of the ordinary, he got back in hit and hit the starter. Pop went the firecracker underneath the car again, and again he got out, opened the hood, and scratched his head. This time, when he got ready to start it, he must have changed his mind in fear he might ruin something if he continued. He just leaned back in the seat. Pop went the third firecracker. This time when he got out he wasn't looking under the hood, he was looking in the bushes for the little no-accounts throwing firecrackers at his new car.

I believe if he had caught one of us, there is no telling just what he might have done. He thought more of the new Hudson than his own wife or even his old hunting dog, bandit. Believe you me, when I say men thought a lot of their dogs that was the straight up truth.

Gary came up with the idea to use the cherry bombs and ten cans to go fishing after that one. His dad used a lot of dynamite on the pipeline that he worked on, blasting rock in order to lay pipe. Several times, he would bring a stick of dynamite home, take it to the river, and set it off in the water. That would shock the fish, bringing them up to float on the top of the water.

So, we boys placed seven cherry bombs in a mason jar, wrapping all the fuses together. After that, we lit a cigarette that we had stolen from my mom. We had all the fuses wrapped around the back of the cigarette, so when it burned down, it would set off all the cherry bombs, knocking out some fish that happened to be swimming by.

We tossed the weighted jar in the river. As it sank, we sat on the shore, waiting for it to go off. When it did, there was an explosion. It looked like one of us boys had been swimming and passed a little gas. There was only one bubble about the size of a small softball that came up.

R.J. BURROUGHS

Chapter 26

That whole fishing thing being a wash out, we thought we might set off a couple packs of black cats near where the girls played next to the swings in the park.

That didn't work out all too well either. Trying to sneak up on a bunch of girls in an open area, though, was about as easy as passing a kidney stone. As usual, I wasn't sure how hard it was to pass a kidney stone, but, according to Mr. Strange who works the elevator at the bank, it is about the hardest thing known to mankind.

He was telling a couple of the guys at the bank entrance that he had passed a kidney stone a couple of nights before. He said it was about as big as one of them black diamond watermelons that a fellow could pick up at the Rush Spring's Watermelon festival in August.

He said it had been hurting him for several weeks. The doctor told him that he would, more than not, pass it one day when he least expected it. The worse thing he said was that the darn thing made him feel like he was going to die each and every time he had to go to the John. Not some of the time, but each and every time.

He went on to say that it felt like one of them Indians who lived near bouts took one of their scalping knives and drove it into him, red hot. It got so bad that he didn't drink anything for days on in, hoping he wouldn't have to go to the bathroom too often.

It got to hurting him so bad that he knew he had to do something. He didn't have the money for an operation to remove it. There was only one thing that he could do if he had any hopes at all of ever being shut of the pain. Mr. Strange was sure no drinking man. We all knew that as much as he preached against it. There were countless times that I remembered where he would talk bad about the problems it caused in Charlie's family, meaning mostly Charlie's mom.

Everyone knew Mr. Strange asked Charlie's mom to get married back when they were both teens. She told him she would be glad to marry him just as soon as Adolph Hitler converted to Judaism. I think he was glad deep down inside, because, even then, she had a hell of a drinking problem.

The day he wanted to relieve himself, Mr. Strange bought himself one whole case of beer, a pint of some kind of whiskey, set on his couch, and started drinking. He drank, I was told, about sixteen of them beers. When he just couldn't hold it any longer, he up and drank half the whiskey. Running to the bathroom, he let her rip. He said the pain was something awful, even with all the beer and whiskey in his system. He grabbed hold of the two pipes running up the wall. Screaming in pain, he pulled the pipes from the wall, causing hot and cold water to blow out the broken pipes. As water started filling the whole room, the kidney stone shot from him, hitting the wall so hard that it made a small round hole in the plaster.

The kidney stone gone, but the beer and whiskey were still in him, he headed down town to tell his friends at the bank. Before he made it there, he was picked up for public drunkenness because his pants were still halfway around his ankles. The whispers reached everyone about the big smile that was on his face as he cleaned up the park the next day.

Chapter 27

When all else failed, we boys got to talking about what we should do with the eleven tin can firecrackers we had left. Jake and Gary wanted to blow up mail boxes. We nixed that idea because of what would happen if anyone ever found out about that one. Jimmy Bric was one thing, but my Grandma could do some damage as well if she heard about me destroying personal property. Something sneakier was in store for us, something we could do far in the sly so no one would ever know about it.

We boys had heard the war veterans talk a lot about the war, how everything was bad in war. However, the worst thing they had to put up with was the booby traps that the enemy always left in different places.

So, hearing all these stories, we boys thought it would be real funny if we could set some kind of a booby trap in the girls bathroom to scare the peewaddley out of them. We had no plans to hurt anyone, but a good scare was something we lived for.

We snuck into school through the math teacher's window. Mrs. Petters' window faced the school court yard and only had half a lock on it with no screen. Several times, the janitor had tried to fix the lock, but the wood was so worn out that he couldn't get another lock to hold. I guess, after trying several times, he just gave up; however, he did put an empty green bean can on top of the window, filled with marbles. I guess he figured, if someone tried to open the window, the green bean can would fall off, making all kinds of noise when it hit the brown tile floor.

The only thing he didn't take into consideration was that everyone who lived in Verden, or at least anyone living in Verden that had a reason to get inside of the school, knew about the green bean can.

We slid the window up really slowly to not set off the alarm. After we all got past, we boys made our way past the trophy case, past several classrooms, and finally reached the girls bathroom. We knew there was no one in there; however, young boys getting ready to enter the girls bathroom was kind of like entering no-man's land. It was like entering into another realm, a place unexplored by twelve-year-old boys. We boys could only imagine what went on in there, what the girls were talking about, and if their talking involved one or all of us at different times.

Gary decided one afternoon before that he was just going to walk right up to the door, push it open, walk in there, and say something like, "Girls, not to worry. I'm only here as a representative of the boys, checking out the décor."

However, when it came time for him to make his grand entrance into the bathroom, he came up with more excuses in a couple of seconds than I could have given in an hour or - for that matter - a day.

He said things like, "What if I open the door and one of them girls is standing there naked as the day she was born? They might think I am one of them perverts."

Either way, the time had finally come and no excuses could or would be made. The day had come for us to finally find out what was in that mysterious place. As we entered the bathroom, we weren't sure what we were going to see or what we were going to do with our firecrackers. After all the work sneaking in, we figured out that none of us knew how to set up one of them booby traps. That and, if we set them off and ran, the ruckus we caused was sure to get everyone in town to the school faster than you could say, "You boys are gonna get a beating."

We decided that the best thing to do would be to just look around, see what it was that made the girls all run in here before and after class to spend their time giggling.

Seeing nothing strange about the place, we all came to the conclusion that there just had to be something wrong with girls to make them act the way they acted. There sure as heck wasn't anything in here to make them act so strange.

As we were leaving, though, we saw some writing on the old, worn-out, gray door leading into the last bathroom stall. Taking a closer look in the dim light, all the other boys broke out in laughter. There, written in large letters, was "Sonny and Daisy." Someone had taken the time to go over it several times with a number two pencil so it would be seen by anyone who happened to pass by.

I knew, as any twelve-year-old boy knew in this situation, that my life had just become more complicated than it had ever been. I would never live those four little words down. I reached deep into my inner thoughts to explain this away.

"That's just crap. One of them dumb old girls wrote that there just to tease Daisy," I said, looking around, hoping to find an ally somewhere in the bunch of boys. They were all smiling stupidly back at me, though.

"One of them might just have written that on there just to tease me and her. Maybe they saw me talking to her at the ball game that time," I said, not believing a word of what I was saying to them myself.

"Sure, one of them did that just to tease you. You make it in here a lot?" Charlie managed to spit out between bouts of laughter.

Why had we come in here? I was wondering to myself. The only thing we accomplished was to embarrass me and give the guys something to tease me about until I was old enough to leave town forever.

Secretly, I think I kind of liked the message, but not their horrible teasing. I was hoping deep down inside that Daisy had written it, not some girl just teasing her like the guys did me. I guess, from that day on, I looked at Daisy as a man or as a boy at least in love.

We all snuck out the same way we snuck in. We went our separate ways to meet up again the next day. We talked about what we should have done while we were in there. What we should have done at this time or that was always an afterthought the next day. It was as if we all lay awake at night thinking of things we should have done.

What I should have done was sneak in there and wipe that 'Sonny and Daisy' off that door before the guys saw it. That was what I should have done. Then at least, I could enjoy this new feeling without the torment that joined it.

EPILOGUE

A couple of the seniors got a clerk to sell them some beer at one of the small mom-and-pop stores in one of the towns several miles away.

All the senior boys decided to start something called the Friday night drinking association, there being only eleven boys in the senior Class they invited all nine girls in their class, thinking that was still not enough to have a good association meeting they invited the entire school,

That Friday night they all met at the park, there was a small amphitheater that someone had built several years before, actually it was nothing more than an old foundation that had been poured to set a statue on. I believe it was a statue of some guy that did something. I'm not sure. However I believe it was to be a statue of a guy called Siros B. Uptagrade. Seems Mr. Uptagrade was the first man in Oklahoma to be killed and scalped by a group of marauding Indians.

After pouring the base for the statue some of the town folks living back then decided getting yourself killed and scalped by Indians wasn't really that much of a big deal. It sure wasn't a big enough deal to get yourself a statue made.

Besides if they put up statues of all the men that got themselves scalped around here, there wouldn't be enough room in the park. So they nixed that idea. That's when they started calling it an 'ampa theater.'

One of the seniors boys, David Cockerham looked a lot like Jesus. Well at least what the picture of Jesus looked like on the wall of the Baptist Church in town— he had long hair and a beard, well at least a goatee. When he stood next to the picture he looked just like what the artist thought Jesus looked like.

I'm told he had several good times with that picture.

That Friday evening the senior boys were drinking their beer when they started feeling the effects of the alcohol. David got up on the amphitheater stage and started preaching, kind of in a low voice to start, then he started screaming things like he heard the preacher at the many revivals our town had.

"You all you sinners out there! You just have to do some repenting, and you got to repent today. Not tomorrow, not next week, but today, today here and now," he screamed to the crowd.

"You got to see the light! People see the light! Look, see the light," he was hollering

"People, look at me, I've sinned. I was once a sinner. I was bad, plum bad through and through," he screamed. "Not now, no not now! I am healed! I have seen the light! I have walked the path of sinners. I have lusted after women. I have lusted after money, lusted after cars, lusted after fun. Not now! Now I am a whole person. Now I have been found. Now I am righteous," he said pointing into the crowd.

"Who among you have not sinned, who out there is not a sinner," He still pointed at no one unparticular.

There were some grownups milling around the park, I guess just to have something to do. There wasn't all that much to do in Verden that time of day, week, or even the year. Hearing the preaching, as much as it was, they strolled over to get a better view.

"Boys, girls, children, come to me let me heal you, let me drudge all the old sins out of you, let me make you whole just as I am, please sinners, come forth, come forth and get whole, get them awful sins washed away." Dan was hollering to the crowd.

"Who among you will be the first! Who among you will come to me? That's it, get off you butts. Get to your feet, and get healed!" He screamed.

"I will, I will, please I will," Jimmy Johnson said, standing up raising his arms to the sky. "I will Preacher! I'm among you and I will," he screamed.

Jimmy Johnson reached down on the ground next to him, picking up a set of crutches; he started making his way to the stage, barley able to walk, more dragging himself then walking with the help of the crutches. Jimmy Johnson was one of the star basketball players on our high school team; there was nothing more wrong with him than there were any of the other boys in town.

When Jimmy reached the stage, David reached down, placing his hand on his head, picked up a beer that was beside him, and started pouring it over Jimmy's head.

"Heal, you sorry, dirty sinner! Heal, get out of this boy you sins you! Free him from his lustful ways! Heal, heal, heal," David shouted, throwing his arms this way and that, looking like a boy that had gone completely mad.

With that, Jimmy screamed at the top of his lungs, threw his crutches in the air, and started dancing around in front of the stage. "I'm healed! I'm healed! Look at me people, I can walk, I can dance, I'm healed!"

Then came Tram Michell, pushing Frank Elliott in an old wheelchair. The front right wheel was shaking back and forth, looking like it would stop working completely or fall off before Tram could get it up to the stage.

When he finally did reach the stage, pushing the worn out chair, David again reached down and grabbed Frank's head, screaming, "Look! Look people! Look at this poor soul. This hunk of human sin—a sinner that was hurt while running from some young girl's father!"

"Heal, sinner, heal," Jimmy screamed at the top of his lungs. "Heal!"

With that Frank jumped from the chair, screaming, "Yes, yes I feel it! I feel it in my arms! My legs! I feel it all over." He started doing a little dance around his wheelchair, singing at the top of his lungs.

This went on for the better part of an hour, or until the seniors either ran out of steam or beer—not sure which came first.

It didn't take long before what happened that evening got around town. A lot of people thought it was funny, dismissed it as

159

just a bunch of shenanigans by kids. However when the preacher found out about it he called the boys and their parents in for a talk. They all said how sorry they were, but if you go to Verden each year around the time school starts, you might just run into the yearly healing session the senior boys carry on each year.

Yes, I will admit that when my time came to start my senior year, I had a hard time finding a wheelchair, but a set of crutches came easy.

ABOUT THE AUTHOR

R. J. was born in Oklahoma City, Oklahoma, in 1946. He attended no less than a dozen elementary schools as his family traveled, working with the pipeline, finally settling in Chickasha Oklahoma . R.J. After Graduating high school in 1965, he spent four years in the U.S. Navy. After leaving Uncle Sam he worked his way up in construction to the position of civil superintendent, the field he still works in to date.